HEARTS
WORLDS
APART

LOVE IN THE TIME OF WAR

Cover and interior design by Ian Koviak

ISBN 979-8-9987018-0-1(paperback)

ISBN 979-8-9987018-1-8 (hardcover)

ISBN 979-8-9987018-2-5 (eBook)

First Edition

Published 2025 by Teresa Ornedo

TERESA MANNING ORNEDO

HEARTS WORLDS APART

LOVE IN THE TIME OF WAR

ACKNOWLEDGMENTS

In loving memory of my father,
Patrick John Manning
(1931-2017)

To my parents, thank you for inspiring me to write this book. It was through my cherished childhood memories and the stories they shared that I was able to develop the characters in this novel.

I also want to thank my wonderful husband, Rene, for his patience and guidance in helping me review the final draft of this book and for encouraging me to reach the finish line.

To all my family and friends, thank you for your support and valuable feedback. Your encouragement has been steadfast. I'm truly grateful for your insight beyond words.

CONTENTS

CHAPTER I

Berlin – October 1944

The headquarters of the Abwehr, Germany's military intelligence service, received an unexpected visit from the SS, a paramilitary organization of Nazi Germany. As people went about their morning routines on the streets, they were suddenly interrupted by the sound of a large group of SS troops marching by, their boots pounding on the pavement, drawing the attention of curious onlookers. One could almost feel the concrete beneath their feet vibrate from the aftershock of the men's boots as they marched in double file along the hard pavement.

Some of the onlookers turned around and hurried off in the opposite direction, while others paused and moved to the side, intrigued by what was happening. As the SS troops marched by, some people automatically and others cautiously followed, raising their right hands and shouting:

"Heil Hitler."

Seeing the SS troops patrolling the streets of Berlin was a familiar sight. People were expected to stop in their tracks and give them the Nazi salute as a sign of respect. If someone didn't do this, it would be viewed as disrespectful to the Führer Hitler, especially given the uncertainty about who was winning the war. Rumors spread that people were disappearing from the streets, never to be seen again. To the surprise of onlookers, the SS troops suddenly changed direction, veering toward the steps and entering the headquarters of the Abwehr. It left bystanders even more curious, wondering what they were doing there. As the SS troops burst through the double doors of the main entrance, they encountered stunned onlookers. Both visitors and workers carried on with their routines - some with briefcases in hand, eager to begin their workday, while others had just wrapped up their shifts and were ready to call it a day.

The foyer buzzed with activity. People entered and exited the elevators while visitors sat in the waiting area, anticipating someone to take them to their destination. Others lingered around, discussing business or exchanging pleasantries. The grand staircase to the upper floor bustled with people eager to bypass the long lines for the crowded elevator. There was a flurry of activity as people hurried back and forth with paperwork, some clutching their files tightly for fear that the documents would scatter everywhere. Others paused to greet one another. But this morning, the sight of an SS officer and his men stopped them in their tracks, leaving them to wonder what the SS were doing here. After all, this was the headquarters of the Abwehr, Germany's military intelligence service. What could the SS possibly want?

The middle-aged male clerk sitting behind the reception desk, directly across from the main entrance of the building, found himself caught off guard by these unexpected guests. At first, he stood abruptly, causing his chair to roll back and collide with the wall. The loud crash reverberated throughout the foyer, stopping people in their tracks as they wondered what was happening. It was almost as if you could hear a pin drop. The clerk stood at attention and saluted the SS officer and his men.

"Heil Hitler," the clerk shouted nervously.

"Heil Hitler," the officer replied.

"Take me immediately to the Foreign Branch department. We have an urgent matter," he demanded.

The clerk felt it was unwise to ask the officer about the urgent matter, so he picked up the phone to inform the department about the visitors. As he did this, his hand shook uncontrollably.

"There's no need to announce our presence right now - take us to the Foreign Branch department right away," the officer insisted.

The SS officer turned and signaled some of his men to remain downstairs while directing the others to follow him.

The clerk felt unprepared. After all, he was responsible for greeting visitors, informing the department about their guests, and guiding them to their destination. In this situation, he recognized that this was a serious issue beyond his control.

"What are we waiting for? Hurry up - we don't have all day," the officer said, clicking his heels impatiently.

The clerk cautiously stepped away from the comfort of his desk and proceeded toward the staircase with the SS officer and his men in tow.

Suddenly, the clerk found himself sweating heavily, with the armpits of his shirt soaked. To make matters worse, sweat from his forehead started trickling toward his eyebrows. With a trembling hand, the clerk reached into his pocket and pulled out a handkerchief to wipe the sweat from his brow. He felt anxious but thought it was best not to show any signs of weakness, even though he knew the officer had already noticed. The clerk led the officer and his men up the winding staircase and down a long, wide hallway until they reached the double doors of the Foreign Branch Department. As the clerk reached for the door, the officer placed his hand on the clerk's shoulder, stopping him in his tracks.

"We'll handle it from here; please return to your desk," he said.

As the clerk was about to leave, he stood at full attention and, instinctively, as if by natural reflex, raised his hand:

"Heil Hitler," he said.

"Heil Hitler," the officer replied.

The clerk turned and walked away without looking back, relieved to put some distance between himself and the SS officer and his men, though he felt uneasy about what was ahead.

CHAPTER 2

The Arrests

The SS officer commanded four of his men to stand guard in the hallway.

"Under no circumstances is anyone allowed to leave or enter through these doors," he instructed.

The SS officer, accompanied by six of his men, entered through the double doors, their guns cocked and ready for action. Seeing the unexpected presence of the SS officer and his men, people stopped in their tracks, wondering what they were doing there! The SS officer commanded everyone to cease their activities and insisted on the department head's presence. Meanwhile, some of his men moved from room to room, ushering staff members out of their offices and guiding them into the large conference room. There was a lot of confusion, and people were anxious about their presence.

Once everyone had gathered, the SS officer stood quietly, as if lost in thought, contemplating what to say next. He slowly removed his gloves and handed them to the subordinate beside him. A sense of unease grew among the staff members as they stood silently, their instincts signaling that this was not good!

"Which of you is the supervisor?" the SS officer demanded.

An elderly man stepped forward, breaking the tense moment.

"Heil Hitler. Officer Kurt Braemer, at your service. How can I assist you and your men today?" he inquired.

The SS officer looked at Kurt with clear condescension. He then pulled a piece of paper from his pocket and held it up high for everyone to see. As he did this, he scanned the room to ensure he had everyone's full attention before turning his focus back to Kurt.

"I'm sure you're all curious about why we're gracing you with our presence today," the SS officer said.

"Here in my hand is a list of twenty-five names of those involved in the July 20 plot, Operation Valkyrie, an assassination attempt on our Führer Hitler," he continued.

The SS officer paused for a moment and looked around the room.

"Without a doubt, a failed attempt to overthrow our government and negotiate peace with our sworn enemies, the British," he said.

The SS officer suddenly thrust the list of names into Kurt's hands. Kurt stood there, at a loss for words.

"Call out the names on the list. Whoever's name is called, please step forward. If you don't, there will be serious consequences!" he warned.

When Kurt saw his name at the top of the list, his demeanor shifted to one of disbelief. The SS officer noted Kurt's reaction and ordered him to call out the names on the list.

"Officer Kurt Braemer," he spoke softly.

"Louder," the SS officer said impatiently.

"Officer Kurt Braemer," Kurt said more loudly.

As he called out his name, Kurt's voice trembled. He couldn't believe he was accused of being involved in the July 20 plot. He was in shock. His whole world suddenly came crashing down. He struggled to regain his composure, but rage soon set in.

"This is outrageous! What is the meaning of this? Such false accusations! I demand to see your commanding officer!" he ordered.

The SS officer seized Kurt by the scruff of his neck, aimed his gun at Kurt's right temple, and pulled the trigger. It was like Russian Roulette; on the first click, nothing happened, but a shot rang out on the second, causing Kurt to collapse to the floor with a loud thud. A loud, piercing scream erupted from a woman as she gasped in horror. Disbelief and horror gripped the room as colleagues watched their supervisor brutally murdered before their eyes. A deadly silence quickly descended upon the room; it felt like time had come to a complete halt. Kurt's lifeless body lay on the floor before them, in a pool of blood oozing from both sides of his temple.

"I advise all of you to cooperate with me unless you want to end up like your colleague here," the SS officer said coldly, waving his gun over Kurt's now lifeless body.

It was evident that the bullet had entered Kurt's right temple at point-blank range and exited through the left side of his temple. As the bullet passed through, it removed a significant portion of his brain, splashing the clothing and feet of those nearby. Many gasped in horror at the sight, feeling powerless to act!

Among the twenty-five names on the list, ten high-ranking officers and several of their staff members were arrested and escorted from their workplace under heavy armed guard, leaving behind stunned colleagues who felt overwhelmed by a situation beyond their control.

As the SS officer and his men descended the grand staircase with their prisoners, they encountered an audience of stunned onlookers. As they stepped through the front double doors into the outside world, they were greeted by passersby going about their daily routines. Some rushed by, too afraid to linger, while others paused to watch as the prisoners were pushed forcefully into the waiting vans, all under heavily armed guard to be taken to the Gestapo headquarters.

Among the first group of ten prisoners was a young officer, Erich Schmidt. He sat there, stunned, wondering what he was being accused of. The plot to kill Hitler! How absurd, he thought to himself. He couldn't believe this was happening; it felt like a bad dream, yet it was real! He could only assume this was an attempt to tarnish and eliminate their organization.

CHAPTER 3

Erich

Erich felt a knot in his stomach, knowing that being on the wrong side of the Gestapo was a bad situation. He was all too aware of this because, in 1934, he started his career with the Gestapo. His job involved conducting background checks on individuals brought in, primarily criminals, communists, and anyone considered a threat to the Third Reich. Two years into the job, Erich became disillusioned as he noticed that people were being held against their will, especially those accused of anti-government sentiment with little or no evidence. Some prisoners endured brutal beatings and torture, while others were sent to prison camps from which there was no return. But today, of all days, Erich and twenty-four of his colleagues found themselves on the wrong side of the Gestapo, accused of participating in the July 20 plot, an attempt on Hitler's life, a crime in which he had no part. Confronted with the unknown, Erich feared what was to come.

Upon arriving at the Gestapo headquarters, prisoners were confronted by heavily armed agents who ordered them to exit the vans.

As the doors swung open, Erich was momentarily blinded by the sudden burst of midday sunlight. Shielding his eyes from the glare, he was unexpectedly yanked from the van with great force.

"Schnell schnell" the SS agent shouted.

"Was that really necessary!" Erich snarled.

From the corner of his eyes, Erich saw the SS officer who had arrested them earlier now standing off to the side, observing the prisoners as they were unloaded from the vans. Shortly afterward, the SS officer and his men left. A Gestapo officer took charge and commanded the prisoners to line up in a single file.

One of Erich's associates, a senior officer, suddenly became enraged.

"Someone's head is going to roll for this! Do you know who you're dealing with?" he shouted.

"We are the Abwehr, and we demand your respect!" he added.

The Gestapo officer approached the prisoner, faced him squarely, and glared directly at him.

"Yes, I know who you are; you're just a piece of shit on my shoes," he said.

As he uttered those words, the prisoner spat directly in the Gestapo officer's face.

The Gestapo officer stepped back, momentarily unsure of how to react. He took a deep breath, reached into his pocket for a handkerchief, and calmly wiped the saliva from his face.

Erich noticed the Gestapo officer's face turn red with anger. Suddenly, the officer punched the prisoner in the stomach, causing him to double over in pain. The prisoner felt as if the air had been knocked out of him, taking his breath away and causing him to buckle at the knees. Just as he was about to fall, Erich and another prisoner instinctively broke their comrade's fall by grabbing him by the arms and holding him upright.

The Gestapo officer stepped back a bit and looked down the line of prisoners.

"Oh, you have no idea what's coming your way," he said.

He paused for a moment, as if contemplating what to say next.

"Oh, you'll get what's coming to you - all of you, traitors. You're a disgrace to the Third Reich," the officer said.

The officer then ordered his agents to take the prisoners away.

Under heavily armed guard, the prisoners were led across a large courtyard, with the Gestapo officer following closely behind. For Erich, it felt surreal to be a prisoner at the Gestapo headquarters. His gut instinct told him he wouldn't be seeing the light of day for a while! Each prisoner was asked to sign their name in a ledger and submit their belongings.

Erich emptied his pockets and handed over his wallet. When it came to his watch, he felt a knot in his stomach. Since the watch had belonged to his father, it was an heirloom he treasured. Erich knew that once he took it off, the chances of seeing it again were zero. When it was time to remove his wedding band, he hesitated even more. The Gestapo agent standing before him noticed his hesitation.

"Schnell, schnell, we don't have all day," he said.

Erich suddenly felt a sharp jab from the butt of a rifle against his shoulder blades, causing him excruciating pain. He had a strong urge to turn around and punch the Gestapo agent in the face, but he thought better of it. After everyone submitted their items, they were given a bundle of old, threadbare clothing and well-worn shoes. Then, they were led into a room and told to change immediately. The Gestapo officer who had overseen the prisoners saluted his fellow officer, leaving him in charge.

The Gestapo officer stood in the corner of the room, watching the prisoners as they changed into the clothing provided for them. Erich noticed that the officer wore an expression that suggested he would prefer to be anywhere else rather than endure the tedious task of watching a group of prisoners hesitantly remove their clothing. Erich was certain this agent had supervised this task countless times. Still, this situation was different; the prisoners he was now overseeing were from the Abwehr headquarters, who were being accused of involvement in the July 20 plot to assassinate Hitler.

The worn clothing Erich now wore sharply contrasted with what he had worn earlier. He found it demoralizing and disrespectful to be stripped of his nice, crisp uniform - one he was proud to wear. The fly of his trousers was broken, and the collar of his shirt was stained with old sweat. Upon closer inspection, Erich suspected that the stains on the front of his shirt were likely old blood, and just the thought of it made him feel nauseous. The jacket was too small for his large frame, with well-worn elbows and a length that stopped two inches above his wrists. The shoes on Erich's feet were a little too tight for his wide feet, and the soles were so thin that he could feel the cold from the concrete floor traveling right up through him.

Erich knew all too well that the clothes on his back and the shoes on his feet belonged to some poor soul who never made it out alive. He imagined this unfortunate person being held against his will during intense interrogation, tied to a chair, and beaten to death with paddleboards. Finding himself on the wrong side of the Gestapo, like countless others who had passed through these very rooms, sent shivers down Erich's spine - it felt surreal. The idea of not knowing what would happen to them terrified him! The Gestapo officer jolted Erich out of his reverie.

"Now look at all of you. You're nobody, just scum," he said, spitting on the floor.

After Erich and his fellow prisoners changed, they stood for a moment, staring down at their uniforms on the floor. Once everyone had changed, the Gestapo officer banged on the door, and shortly after, ten Gestapo agents appeared.

"Take them away," the officer ordered.

The Gestapo agents escorted the prisoners down a long, dark, narrow corridor. Their mood was somber as they trudged silently in an orderly single file. Each prisoner was pushed into his assigned cold, dark, damp cell. Erich, the last in line, hesitated momentarily, feeling exhausted, defeated, and at a loss for words.

"Schnell, schnell," one of the Gestapo agents said coldly.

The agent shoved the butt of his gun into the middle of Erich's shoulder blades, sending him tumbling into his cell and causing him to land on his hands and knees. Erich heard the heavy metal door slam shut behind him, as the Gestapo agent stood on the other side snickering while locking it. Erich felt nothing but humiliation from the disrespect shown to him by this agent. He rose slowly from the ground, feeling his anger surge as his face burned with rage and his hands instinctively clenched into tight fists. He desperately wanted to bang his fists against the door and scream, "You bastard," but his inner voice urged him to take a deep breath. Eric and the Gestapo agent locked eyes briefly, but only contempt was reflected in the agent's gaze. Then, he turned and walked away, vanishing into the darkness of the corridor. All Erich could hear was the echo of the Gestapo agent's heavy boots and the jingle of keys by his side. The sound of heavy steel doors slamming shut soon followed, accompanied by the retreating footsteps of the other Gestapo agents and the clinking of their keys, echoing through the narrow corridor, soon giving way to silence.

Erich felt isolated and alone in a cold, dark, damp cell, anxious about what the next day would bring. From the moment they were arrested until they arrived at the Gestapo headquarters, they encountered nothing but disdain. Erich knew that the officers involved in the July 20 plot had already been executed and that their families had been sent to internment camps. Even months later, arrests continued, and now Erich and his fellow prisoners are in the basement of the Gestapo headquarters, waiting for their fate!

CHAPTER 4

The Trial

Erich and five others stood in the dock, anxiously awaiting their fate. They stood quietly, dressed in worn clothes that they had worn day and night for the past ten days, and now they smelled strongly of body odor. Erich felt embarrassed, as neither he nor the others had bathed or shaved in almost two weeks. He realized that this was the Gestapo's tactic to demoralize them and make them feel worthless.

"I won't let those bastards win," his inner voice told him.

Despite his life hanging in the balance, Erich stood in the dock with his head held high. The worst-case scenario he could imagine was receiving a death sentence. To Erich's surprise, he discovered that the head of his department, who stood next to him alongside several senior officers, had been caught communicating directly via radio with the London Secret Service. In exchange for their services, the British government offered them the chance to start anew in a country of their choice. Fortunately, Erich and two of his colleagues were spared execution because there wasn't enough evidence against them.

"Not guilty," the Judge said.

Erich sighed in relief when he heard the verdict of "Not guilty," feeling an immense weight lift off his shoulders. The deafening sound of drums rolling in his head while he awaited the Judge's verdict now faded away.

"This court finds you not guilty of direct association with the July 20 plot. However, due to your close ties to the head of your department, this court finds you guilty by association; therefore, we sentence you to a life of imprisonment at an undisclosed location," the judge announced.

Erich was left speechless upon hearing the judge's sentence of life imprisonment. Meanwhile, the judge continued sentencing the others.

"This court finds you guilty. At the command of our Führer Hitler and the Third Reich, you are to be removed from this location and taken back to the Gestapo Headquarters. There, you will be hanged by the neck, to die a slow and agonizing death, and God will have no mercy," the judge said.

The prisoners gasped in disbelief upon hearing their sentencing.

"Furthermore, due to your actions, your family will endure hardship. Your property will be confiscated, and your family will be taken to an undisclosed prison location," he concluded.

Erich felt a chill run down his spine and shuddered at the thought of being on the receiving end of those words. He felt sympathy for the unfortunate prisoners and the impact it would have on their families. One thing was clear: he was thankful that his wife, Maud, and his grandparents had managed to leave Germany. Erich was concerned about their safety, particularly due to the relentless bombing raids on Berlin both day and night. He shuddered at the thought of their situation had they stayed. What if?

It had been nearly two years since Maud and his grandparents left with the help of Erich's close and trusted friend, Karl Weber. With the right connections, Karl arranged for their safe passage: first, his grandparents to Switzerland and then Maud to Ireland. Saying goodbye to Maud was the hardest part; it felt as if someone had ripped his heart out and torn it in two. He felt relieved when he received a telegram from Maud confirming her safe arrival in Ireland; however, that was the last time he heard from her. But today, of all days, as Erich faces a lifetime of imprisonment, he feels his hope of ever seeing his family again slipping away.

Erich believed that he and his colleagues were being used as scapegoats due to the government's overwhelming paranoia at a time when Germany faced a strong possibility of losing the war. All he could think about was how foolish he was for remaining loyal to the Third Reich and for what? Now he faced a life sentence for a crime he had no part in. It made him question the judicial system, which was both unfair and unjust! Being found guilty by association, Erich shuddered at the thought of Maud and his grandparents being rounded up and sent to a prison camp, just like the families of the men who had just been sentenced to death.

Since the July 20 plot of 1944, a widespread witch hunt has targeted anyone associated with the attempt to overthrow Hitler and the

Third Reich. The previous year was disastrous for the Third Reich as they fought a losing battle against the Russians. Their biggest setback occurred when the Russians defeated them at Stalingrad in February 1943. The consensus was that Germany was losing the war, and people's morale was at an all-time low. Additionally, this was a dangerous time when no one felt safe sharing their opinions, not even with their closest friends.

Erich felt that these days he could trust no one, let alone voice his opinions. Too many people were reporting on each other - neighbors, friends, and even family members! He understood that people were hungry and would go to great lengths for an extra ration card. Then there were families trying to get their loved ones out of prison by using information as a bargaining chip for their freedom. Some people vanished, never to be seen again; rumors suggested they were either sent east to fight against the Russians or court-martialed and executed. Erich learned through the grapevine that his good friend, Karl Weber, was caught aiding Jews at the end of 1942. As punishment, he was sent to the front lines to fight the Russians, only to die shortly thereafter.

Erich reminded himself to stay focused and to stay alive. All he could hope for was to keep his sanity intact and for this God-forsaken war to end. The only thing keeping him going was the thought of Maud and the hope that they would be reunited one day.

CHAPTER 5

Erich - 1937

Erich Schmidt, a Berliner, was the son of an Irish mother and a German father. His parents were tragically killed in a car accident when he was just ten years old. At twenty-six, he stood at six feet, three inches, with pale blue eyes and curly, dark brown hair. He bore a scar on his right cheek, a reminder of a fencing duel from his university days. Dueling without protective masks was common among young, upper-class German men eager to prove their masculinity. He took pride in his scar, seeing it as a source of his strength. Erich was charismatic, yet despite his charm and the distinctive scar on his right cheek, some people found him intimidating, especially as a Gestapo agent.

After more than two years of working for the Gestapo, Erich became disillusioned. His role involved overseeing background checks on individuals, predominantly criminals, communists, and those deemed a threat to the Third Reich. His primary concern was that more people than usual were being brought in for questioning. Individuals were being arrested, often taken from their homes in the middle of the night and, in some cases, in broad daylight. Much of the evidence against these individuals was based on expressed opinions, merely comments they made in public, or the word of a disgruntled neighbor eager to see the last of them. For many, they faced accusations of promoting communist ideology or being anti-fascist, both of which were considered enemies of the Third Reich.

Erich was acutely aware that for many of these individuals, there was little to no evidence of the crime they were accused of. Many were held involuntarily, and many endured beatings and torture, even to the brink of death. Additionally, since the passing of the Nuremberg Laws in 1935, which prohibited interracial relationships between Jews and non-Jews, as this was viewed as a form of racial pollution of the German race, thousands of Berliners were found guilty of such crimes and arrested.

The enactment of the Nuremberg Laws established that relationships and marriages between an Aryan German and a Jew were illegal. Suddenly, German civilians discovered for the first time that their connections with their wives, husbands, or loved ones were no longer recognized. Negative posters plastered the streets, making everyone aware of the new laws. As a result of these regulations, the Jewish community was marginalized and forced into isolation.

Shortly after the Nuremberg Laws were enacted, a wave of suicides soon followed. For the first time, people were realizing their identity as part of the Jewish race - a Jew with no rights! Jewish business owners soon faced boycotts, losing the customers they had known for many years. Many were forced to close or sell their family businesses, which had been run for generations, at substantial discounts. Erich saw numerous shops, businesses, and department stores marked with the yellow Star of David, some displaying "Juden" in large letters across their windows. Shortly thereafter, Jews were expelled from their jobs, schools, and universities and were banned from entering local entertainment venues, such as restaurants, theaters, swimming pools, and parks. Yellow benches in parks were labeled "For Jews Only."

Witnessing the drastic changes and mistreatment of Jewish people in his beloved city of Berlin, Erich found it deeply troubling. These recent events confirmed Erich's disillusionment not only with the Gestapo but also with the Third Reich. Rumors circulated at work from upper management about a series of executions targeting political opponents of the regime. Erich had considered that during such turbulent times, he might become implicated. Even though he didn't share Hitler's views or those of the people around him, he kept his opinions to himself. Erich felt that he could trust no one in the workplace and sensed that everyone was looking out for themselves.

In an unexpected turn of events, Erich was approached by the Abwehr, Germany's military intelligence service, which offered him a position as one of their agents. Because of his Irish heritage, he was viewed as the ideal candidate to be part of a covert sleeper cell in Ireland.

"I see you have Irish roots. Our records show that your mother was Irish. Therefore, you have a grandmother named Margaret and her brother Patrick, your granduncle, in Ireland," the agent said.

"Yes, this makes you an ideal candidate for what we have in mind," he added.

Erich was both speechless and pleasantly surprised.

"We want you to be part of a sleeper cell. You know, go there, live there, observe the political climate, and, most importantly, find out how the citizens of Ireland feel about us. We want to know if we will have the cooperation of the Irish people when the time comes for a German invasion of Great Britain," the agent emphasized.

"As you know, the relationship between the Irish and the British is not a healthy one; they resent those Brits just as much as we do! So, I believe we're onto something here," he stressed.

After hearing this information, Erich struggled to comprehend what he had just learned. Being part of a sleeper cell in Ireland was one thing, but deceiving his mother's family was an entirely different matter. After all, it had been sixteen years since he had last seen his grandmother and granduncle. He was only ten years old when he spent his last summer on the farm with his parents, and shortly after returning to Berlin, his parents were tragically killed in a horrific car accident. Two months after the funeral, his father's parents sent him to boarding school, marking the end of those long summer months in Ireland.

Erich felt he had limited options, especially given the volatile environment he was living in. One thing was clear: he was grateful for this opportunity, which would distance him from the political drama surrounding him. It was time to put pen to paper.

CHAPTER 6

Ireland - 1937

To Patrick's surprise, the postman delivered a letter from Germany addressed to him and Margaret. It was from his grandnephew, Erich Friedrich Smyth.

"Can you believe it? It's a letter from your grandson," Patrick said.

Margaret stood at the kitchen sink, washing the morning dishes. After drying her hands, she joined Patrick at the kitchen table.

"Did I just hear you say we received a letter from Erich?" she exclaimed.

Patrick read the letter aloud.

"September 7th, 1937

Dear Margaret and Patrick,

This is Erich. It's been a long time since we saw each other, back when I was just a ten-year-old boy. So much time has passed since then. Now, as an adult, I long to see you both again and revisit my fond childhood memories of those long summer days spent on the farm with my parents and you.

I plan to take a leave of absence from work early next year and would love to visit you in March.

If it's okay with you, I would like to stay with you for a while. Perhaps I could be of some help to you on the farm.

Yours truly

Erich Friedrich Smyth"

Margaret was thrilled to hear from her grandson, a grown man finally reaching out to her. She took the letter from Patrick and read it over and over again. She couldn't believe that Erich, her only daughter's child, was planning to stay with them for a while. Even though sixteen years had passed, it felt like it was only recently that Erich and his parents had spent their summer vacation with them. Margaret recalled the cherished moments she shared with her daughter and grandson. Tragically, shortly after their return to Berlin, both of Erich's parents, Eileen and Heinrich, were killed in a car crash.

"How was he doing? What was he up to? What did he look like? Would she ever see him again?" she often wondered.

A sudden wave of guilt washed over Margaret as she reflected on all those years lost, missing out on her grandson growing up. She reminded herself that unforeseen circumstances had changed everything. After Erich lost his parents, he was sent to boarding school, which ended his summer visits to Ireland. As an adult, he has reached out and wants to visit them. He can stay as long as he likes.

"You know, Margaret, we're not getting any younger. One thing's for sure: we could do with a pair of extra hands around here," Patrick said, shaking Margaret out of her reverie.

"For sure I hear you," she replied.

"As you know, farm hands are hard to come by these days. God only knows that young men today aren't willing to work for the wages you offer," Patrick said.

"It's no wonder they're heading to England; who could blame them when jobs are few and far between?" Margaret said.

Margaret understood this all too well; she didn't envy today's youth, who face limited job prospects. Their options were either government work or farming, but most jobs in their area were farming. Patrick acknowledged that job opportunities were almost nonexistent in Ireland, where unemployment was at an all-time high. It was no surprise that young people left for England in search of a better life. Over the past two years, he had watched friends' sons and daughters leave, catching the first boat to England. He didn't blame them because they had limited options.

America was once seen as the ideal destination for those seeking a better future with promising job opportunities. However, everything changed with the 1929 stock market crash, which plunged the country into a depression, making it difficult for anyone to migrate there. Upon receiving the letter from his grandnephew about his planned visit, Patrick couldn't have been more thrilled.

For Patrick, Erich's upcoming visit couldn't have come at a better time, especially with all the maintenance needed both inside and outside the house, particularly the roof, which urgently needed repairs. Despite the numerous repairs for leaks and tile replacements, there always seemed to be another problem requiring attention. Over the years, the leaks have caused water damage, evident in rooms with dark, damp patches on the ceilings and wallpaper peeling from the walls. For Patrick, maintaining the old farmhouse felt like a never-ending task. Patrick felt that it had been far too long and put pen to paper:

"October 18th,1937

Dear Erich,

Yes, it has been a long time - too long! Let's not prolong it any further! We are both thrilled to hear from you, and yes, Margaret and I would love to have you. You are welcome to come and stay for as long as you wish.

Don't be a stranger; after all, you are family!

Yours truly,

Patrick and Margaret

PS: We could certainly use an extra pair of hands!"

CHAPTER 7

Ireland – March 1938

Margaret hugged and kissed her grandson, then held him at arm's length to take him in.

"Oh my, look at you - you've grown into a handsome young man," she exclaimed.

"The last time I saw you, you were just a boy," she said.

Margaret stepped back, took a deep breath, and then exhaled softly.

"Sure, you're the spitting image of your mother. You have her eyes and your father's good looks," she added.

Erich noticed his grandmother's eyes welling up with tears.

"Ah sure, enough of that now," Margaret said dismissively.

For a moment, Margaret felt as though she might burst into tears. She struggled to hold back her emotions, her voice betraying her with a slight quiver.

"Oh, if only they could see you now. God rest their souls; what a tragedy," she said.

Seeing her grandson as a man at the age of 26 stirred deep emotions within her, especially the painful memories of losing a loved one who had long since passed. Margaret could no longer hold back the tears - tears for the loss of a loved one and tears of joy at seeing her grandson again!

Patrick, her brother who had been watching the reunion between his sister and her grandson, stepped forward and firmly shook his grandnephew's hand.

"Sure, it's great to see you; it's been far too long," he said.

Sixteen years had passed, and now, as a fully grown man, Erich stood before Margaret and Patrick, wondering where all that time had gone.

Erich was thrilled to be back in Ireland, but this was no ordinary visit; he had been sent on a mission. From the moment he set foot in Ireland, he felt welcomed by the warmth of the Irish people. Reuniting with his grandmother and granduncle truly made him feel at home. Amidst the peace and tranquility of the countryside, he felt the heavy burden lift from his shoulders!

CHAPTER 8

Such Fond Memories

With Erich back in Ireland, his cherished childhood memories came flooding back. Those long summer breaks were the happiest times of his childhood, particularly the special moments he shared with his grandmother. He fondly remembers the haymaking season, helping her bring lunch and flasks of tea to the field workers. Another cherished memory of his grandmother was how she coaxed him out of bed at dawn, just as the rays of sunlight streamed across his bed. Remembering this fond moment made him chuckle. Erich recalls his grandmother taking his hand and guiding him as they quietly tiptoed down the stairs and out of the house.

"We need to be quiet; we don't want to wake the household just yet," she said.

Once outside, they made their way to the garden. As they walked, she explained to Erich how the rising sun affects the plants. Upon arriving at the garden, she knelt and gestured for him to join her.

"Just watch!" she said.

They sat silently, observing the plants gradually unfurl, greeting the morning sunlight. To a ten-year-old child, it was magical. After-ward, Erich assisted his grandmother in feeding the pigs, chickens, and horses. Reflecting on those treasured moments with his grand-mother was priceless.

"Oh, to be a child again, sweet, innocent, and carefree," he thought.

Through a child's eyes, the world was full of mysteries and won-ders, and the sun always shone! Now, sixteen years later, he has returned as an officer of the Third Reich, tasked with a mission to serve as a potential spy.

On his first night in Ireland, Erich slept soundly. It was the best sleep he'd had in a long time. As soon as his head hit the soft pillows, he was out like a light. Erich felt snug and warm, buried deep beneath the blankets and a hot water bottle that Margaret had slipped into his bed earlier. At dawn, he awoke to the sound of a rooster crowing "cock-a-doodle-doo," and shortly thereafter, the sounds of cows followed, mooing and ready to be milked and fed. For a moment, Erich almost forgot where he was; one thing was cer-tain: it was not back in Berlin.

It was music to his ears, a sharp contrast to the unsettling sounds Erich had encountered back in Berlin. At night, he spent countless sleepless hours lying in bed, listening to Berlin come alive with the terrifying distant echoes of shouting, followed by the pounding on doors. Erich couldn't imagine what was going through the minds of those on the other side. Even more unsettling were the eerie, high-pitched screams of terror, soon followed by the sounds of drunken young men stumbling home in the early morning hours, singing and shouting without a care in the world. With the unsettling nightly sounds of Berlin, Erich struggled to drown them out. It was only when he woke up to the sounds of cars and people engaging in their morning routines that he felt at ease. He felt that Berlin had become a lawless society, creating a dangerous environment, especially for the Jewish communities who no longer felt welcomed in German society. A gentle knock from Margaret on his bedroom door pulled him from his reverie.

"Time to get up, young man. Breakfast is getting cold," she said.

Hearing his grandmother's lovely Irish lilt through his bedroom door was music to Erich's ears. He peeked out from under the covers, but the chilly, damp air made him hesitate to leave the warmth of his bed. Suddenly, he caught a whiff of the delicious smells wafting up from the kitchen below. The aroma of freshly baked bread and cooked meat made his mouth water and his stomach growl with hunger – he was ravenous! On the count of one, two, three, Erich threw off the bedcovers and jumped out of bed onto the cold wooden floorboards.

CHAPTER 9

Patrick

For a man in his early seventies, Patrick was impressively strong and healthy, thanks to many years of hard physical labor on the farm that kept him active and in excellent shape. Patrick was the second eldest of four siblings. There would have been five because Patrick's twin brother was stillborn.

From an early age, Patrick often wondered what life might have been like if his twin brother had survived. However, growing up in a household where it was never discussed, he learned to keep his thoughts to himself. He imagined his brother would look just like him, but he sometimes felt sad, sensing that part of him was missing. It wasn't until he was thirteen that his father's mother passed away, prompting his father to reveal the whereabouts of his twin brother's remains. Patrick was also surprised to learn that his father had named his twin brother Joseph.

As the grandmother's coffin was lowered into its final resting place beside her husband, who had passed away fifteen years earlier, Patrick's father spoke about the heartbreaking loss of his twin son. It seemed like it was only yesterday when his father took him aside and pointed his finger toward the far-right corner of the burial plot.

"Look, son, that is where we buried your baby brother, Joseph," his father said.

As a curious child, Patrick asked many questions.

"Why is he buried in the corner, Daddy? And why doesn't he have a headstone like Grannie and Grandad?" he inquired.

"Son, the church wouldn't allow it; since he was stillborn and unbaptized, he is in purgatory," his father replied.

It was shortly after the funeral that Patrick's parents disclosed more to him and his siblings about the loss of their stillborn son.

"I remember now; I was in the waiting room when the doctor approached me with the news that we had twin boys, but only one survived. He informed me that someone would be with me shortly, and he left before I could say anything. About thirty minutes later, the head nurse approached me directly and handed me this small white box containing your brother's remains, advising me to reach out to the local priest for further guidance. She left me standing there speechless."

He paused for a moment as if considering what to say next.

"I left the hospital in a daze, and the only place I could think of was to go straight to the priest's house. To my dismay, the priest informed me that since the baby was stillborn, the Catholic Church did not acknowledge it, and therefore, it was stuck in purgatory and had no place in heaven. As one would say, it was stuck in limbo, so a funeral was out of the question!" he exclaimed, throwing his hands up.

His mother sat silently by her husband's side, holding his hand.

"God willing, I was fortunate to leave the hospital with a baby in my arms, as there were a couple of women in my ward who left empty-handed," she said.

Patrick's father gently squeezed his mother's hand.

"The only place we could think of was to put him in the right-hand corner of the family plot," he said softly.

Patrick vividly recalled his father's voice, filled with emotion, as he sighed deeply while speaking those words. Yet, he composed himself as if it were best not to reveal too much of one's emotions. It was only years later, as a man, that Patrick understood this was his parents' way of coping with their grief over a lost child.

Years later, the family faced another tragedy. Patrick's youngest brother, Sean, just shy of his 21st birthday, died from rheumatic fever. Shortly after Sean's death, Patrick overheard his father expressing to a close friend:

"You can lose a parent, you can lose a sibling, but nothing is worse than losing your child – no words can describe it; it's just goddam awful!"

Patrick noticed that shortly after his brother's passing, his father began drinking heavily and spending long hours at the local pub. He could only assume this was his father's way of dealing with the loss of a son.

When Patrick's parents passed away, his eldest brother, Eamon, stood to inherit the farm. Tragically, Eamon died in an accident on the farm after losing control of his tractor, leaving Margaret and

Patrick as the only surviving siblings. Following Eamon's death, Patrick automatically became the next of kin to inherit the farm.

Patrick never married. At times, he felt as if he were married to the farm, which kept him too busy to think about finding a wife. As a bachelor, he assumed the responsibility of caring for his sister Margaret. Widowed at 22 after losing her husband to tuberculosis, Margaret was left pregnant. Without a husband to support her, Patrick stepped in as a dutiful sibling as he couldn't bear to watch his sister suffer; otherwise, she could have ended up in the poorhouse, and worse, her child given up for adoption to a childless American couple.

Patrick was grateful for what he and Margaret had and felt fortunate; life on the farm was good. They had a stable income by supplying the surrounding areas with milk and butter. They also had their wheat milled by a local farmer and sold the flour to nearby communities. Additionally, they leased horses to local farmers for plowing and occasionally entered them in local races. There was enough income to sustain them. Life was good!

CHAPTER 10

Margaret

Margaret was thrilled that her only grandson, Erich, Eileen's only child, was not just visiting but also planning to stay with them for a while. It felt as if a piece of Eileen had come home! She reminisced about when Eileen left for university in Dublin; it broke her heart to see her little girl moving so far away. To Margaret, it felt like the other side of the world. At the university, Eileen met and fell in love with a German student named Heinrich. Shortly after graduation, they got married and relocated to Berlin, increasing the distance between themselves and Margaret. Tragically, both were taken from this life far too soon, leaving behind a ten-year-old son. The last time Margaret saw Erich was at his parents' funeral in Berlin, where he was just a boy too young to understand the concept of death. Margaret recalled the day she received the telegram from Heinrich's parents; her world came crashing down.

"October 10th, 1921

Dearest Margaret and Patrick,

It is with our deepest sympathy that we regret to inform you of the tragic deaths of your beloved daughter, Eileen, and our dear son, Heinrich. Shortly after their return from Ireland, they were both killed in a car accident on September 20, 1921.

The funeral will be held on October 1st at 10 am at the following address:

43-45 Friedenau Cemetery,

Berlin,

Germany.

Signed

Friedrich and Alexandra Schmidt"

Margaret remembered it was late morning when she got the bad news. She was at the kitchen sink when she noticed the postman approaching the driveway. She opened the door before he could knock and saw the expression on his face that said it all: the bearer of bad news.

"I think you should sit down before you read this, love" he said.

When Margaret read the words "the tragic death of your beloved daughter..." it took her a moment to fully grasp that her daughter had recently passed.

"No, no, not my little girl," and then the ground gave way beneath her.

Patrick was outside at the pig trough feeding the pigs when he heard her screams. He rushed in to find Margaret collapsed and curled up on the floor, in a state of shock. He had to pry the telegram from her tight grip to understand what was happening, as her sobbing was so uncontrollable that she wasn't making sense.

Margaret fondly recalled Patrick embracing her and holding her close.

"A parent should never see their child go before them," Margaret murmured through her sobs.

Margaret reminisced about the day of the funeral. It was cold, wet, and windy, under a dull, dark gray sky with occasional showers. The gathering was small and intimate, attended by Margaret, Patrick, Heinrich's parents, young Erich, and a few close friends.

The funeral procession moved slowly as family and friends walked behind the two horse-drawn hearses, each carrying the coffins of their loved ones toward the church gates. The mourners stood silently to the side, observing as the professional pallbearers - twelve in total, six for each coffin. Each pallbearer donned a classic long black coat, a top hat, and white gloves. They carefully removed the coffins from the hearses and lifted them onto their shoulders. They proceeded through the church entrance, along the pathway, with family and friends closely following behind, guiding them to the final resting place for Eileen and Heinrich, where Heinrich's ancestors had been laid to rest for generations.

Everyone gathered at the gravesite, watching as each coffin was gently lowered into the ground. Margaret was grateful to have Patrick by her side during such a tragic time as she dealt with the pain of losing her only child. She also felt empathy for the suffering that

Heinrich's parents were enduring. Feeling overwhelmed, she wanted to scream about how unfair life seemed.

It was not until after the funeral that Margaret learned from Heinrich's parents that, according to some witnesses, their son had taken a bend too quickly, causing their car to careen off the cliff edge and fall into the deep ravine below. Recovering the bodies took days. To this day, Margaret remained unforgiven of her son-in-law for robbing her of her only daughter and taking both parents away from their son Erich. Losing one parent was difficult enough, but losing both at the same time was a significant loss for a child!

CHAPTER II

Morning Outing

Erich enjoyed a hearty breakfast of black and white puddings, two sausages, two slices of bacon, two eggs, and baked beans. He then had fresh soda bread with thick slices of creamy butter and homemade jam, washed down with a strong cup of tea. Erich felt completely stuffed, to the point that his stomach could burst!

"It looks like a nice dry morning out there – let's go for a bike ride," Patrick suggested to Erich.

"It looks like it's going to be a lovely day after all," Margaret said, glancing out the kitchen window.

Erich joined her at her side, took the dish towel from its hook, and started drying the dishes.

"You don't have to do that, young man. Off with you, you better get ready. Now shoo, I'll take care of this," Margaret said, waving Erich away.

"Okay, Nan," Erich replied with a shrug.

Erich suddenly realized that he might be too old to call her "Nan." After all, he was on a first-name basis with his grandparents on his father's side.

Margaret quickly grasped Erich's train of thought.

"Oh, young man, please call me Nan. After all, I am your grandmother."

"I'm so happy you're here, but you should get going love, while it's nice and dry out there," she said, gently touching Erich's arm.

As Margaret watched her grandson walk away, her heart fluttered a little, and tears of joy filled her eyes. Even though she had lost her only child, seeing Erich as a fine young man reassured her that Eileen's legacy lives on.

As the men were about to leave on their bikes, Margaret rushed out of the house and handed them a packed lunch.

"This will keep you going until dinner time. Now off you go. Enjoy yourselves!" she said.

"God willing, it will hopefully stay dry - we could use more days like this!" she added as an afterthought.

The morning was in their favor: it was dry, with occasional glimpses of sunshine trying to break through the otherwise thick, cloudy sky. In the distance, dark clouds gathered, hinting at the possibility of rain.

"Those dark clouds in the distance - there's a good chance we might get caught in a shower or two. I've packed some rain gear, just in case," Patrick said.

"You definitely can't trust the Irish weather; when it rains, it pours - we can have five seasons in one day!" he added.

Margaret watched Patrick and Erich take off down the driveway on their bikes. Once they were out of sight, she felt the morning dampness chill her to the bone. She quickly closed the door behind her and welcomed the warm comfort of her home.

Patrick and Erich made their way to the nearby village. Erich observed the narrow country roads, especially the low-lying stone walls flanked by overgrown thorny bushes and hedges on both sides. As a child, he learned from his mother that farmers built these stone walls by stacking stones on top of one another without using mortar. The walls defined the boundaries of their farmland and kept their animals from wandering onto the road. Erich also learned that one didn't have to dig very deep to reach these stones; the moment the shovel struck the soil, it uncovered nothing but solid rock beneath the layer of grass.

As an adult, Erich could see miles of stone walls winding across the rolling green hills; it was truly breathtaking. Although Erich spent many summers as a child on the farm, he was too young to truly appreciate its beauty. He noted the differences between the Irish countryside and his homeland. For example, the German countryside featured vast open fields separated only by rows of hedges and trees, while its roads were wider and lined with ditches.

As they approached the nearby village, just a mile from the house, Erich was captivated by the stunning view of a fifteenth-century Abbey, which had long been deserted. The sight of the Abbey reminded Erich of an oil painting. They stopped at the viewpoint and were soon joined by a couple of horses with their young foals in tow. Patrick took some crab apples from his pockets and held them in his palm. As soon as he extended his hand, the horses trotted over.

"The horses love crab apples. Sure, they grow everywhere like weeds, and we have loads of them behind the house. Margaret makes the best mouthwatering apple pies for miles around," Patrick said.

The horses munched contentedly on the apples, and once they were gone, Patrick and Erich stood quietly, gently stroking their heads. With no more apples to feed them, the horses soon trotted off with their foals in tow.

Erich loved horses, but it had been some time since he rode one. He learned to ride during his years at boarding school. At the university, he also had the chance to ride an Arabian horse and go hunting on his best friend's family estate.

"It's breathtaking, isn't it?" Patrick asked, snapping Erich out of his reverie.

Erich completely agreed.

Erich and Patrick stood quietly for a moment, taking in the stunning views of the Abbey.

"Ah, it's one of our pride and joys, founded in the 14th century and established as a Franciscan Abbey a century later. It was built over the foundations of a Norman castle," Patrick said.

"The last monk was buried there in 1820. We can check it out later," he added.

"Yes, I would really like that," Erich replied.

Erich closed his eyes, inhaled the fresh country air, and exhaled slowly, soaking in the peacefulness of the countryside. The combination of neighing horses and the faint, distant barking of dogs contributed immensely to the tranquil harmony of the landscape. For Erich, he couldn't be happier to be in this faraway land, despite the uncertainty of what the future held for him. For now, it felt as if time had come to a complete standstill; it was wonderful! With that, they hopped on their bikes and continued their journey to the local village.

CHAPTER 12

The Local Village

In the village, there was hardly a soul in sight except for a couple of women standing on the street corner, chatting and pausing only to glance at Patrick and Erich as they entered.

"They'll certainly be curious to know who you are, Erich, and it won't take long before they find out," Patrick warned.

"It's nice and quiet right now since most of the villagers are in the fields, except for a few who work for the Civil Service," he added.

Erich noticed a young boy running on the opposite side of the street with a bucket in hand. Soon after, the boy stopped at the street pump to fill the bucket with fresh water. Erich observed with curiosity as the boy used all his strength to pump the water, filling the bucket to the brim. The boy then walked home slowly and carefully, making sure not to spill any water.

Erich observed rows of whitewashed houses with thatched roofs lining both sides of the street. Some of the houses looked like they had seen better days; they appeared quite rundown and in need of repair. Patrick pointed out the store on the left side of the street, pulling Erich out of his reverie.

"This is where we go for a quick shop. Mind you, the items are a bit pricey," Patrick said.

"We usually do most of our shopping in the main town, about five miles that way," Patrick said, gesturing in the direction they came from.

Patrick saw Erich staring at the police station across from the store.

"Ah, the police station and the house next to it are where the village policeman and his family live," Patrick said.

As they neared the end of the street, Patrick felt a surge of excitement when the butcher shop came into view.

"This is where we bring our pigs. It's amazing how much food you can get from just one pig: sausages, bacon, ham, and black and white puddings. There's enough food to last us for quite a while," Patrick said.

Patrick and Erich turned the corner and continued down the next street, where Erich noticed more rows of white thatched-roof houses lining both sides. When they reached the end of the street, they came upon a charming little stone bridge. Patrick pointed to the small building by the river below.

"This is our local village hall, where we hold monthly farmers' meetings. The youth club, Christmas parties, and wedding receptions also take place here," he explained.

"One thing for sure, there's plenty of gossip here. It's what makes the world go round," Patrick said, chuckling.

Erich noticed that his granduncle could speak endlessly without taking a breath. He could barely get a word in, but he understood that his granduncle was thrilled to have him there. Erich was happy to be in Ireland and reconnect with his mother's family. Although he felt mentally drained, he appreciated being in a place where he could relax and unwind.

Patrick and Erich continued their journey across the bridge, coming into full view of the Abbey, which stood majestically, surrounded by acres of land dotted with grazing cows. Next to the bridge was a grotto dedicated to the Virgin Mary, and adjacent to it stood a church. Between the grotto and the church was a gate that provided access to the Abbey. Erich was mesmerized by the statue of the Virgin Mary, who gazed back at him with profound sorrow, her arms outstretched and palms facing upward.

"Bless me, Father, for I have sinned; it has been a long time since my last confession, and the last time I attended Mass was when I was 16," Erich's inner voice said.

Erich vividly recalled being 16; it felt like just yesterday. He remembered his Sunday morning routine: entering the church through the front door and quietly slipping out the back. He would linger on the church grounds until Mass ended, watching the congregation as they departed. Soon after, he would retreat to the sanctuary of his room at the boarding school run by the Christian Brothers. Since his parents' tragic death when he was only ten, this had been his home for the past few years of his youth. The Christian Brothers instilled in him the belief that if he didn't attend church, he would end up in hell - a place of eternal damnation!

"Such Catholic guilt," Erich thought to himself.

Patrick gestured toward the church, shaking Erich out of his reverie.

"This is where Margaret and I go to church on Sundays, rain or shine. You're more than welcome to join us," he said.

"I respect your decision if you don't want to; it's totally your choice," he added as an afterthought.

Suddenly, a pang of guilt washed over Erich for having those thoughts a moment ago. Was it just the Catholic guilt?

"Sure, I'd be happy to join you," Erich said.

"We should get going; it's almost noon, and we have much to see," Patrick suggested.

As they left the village, Erich noticed there were five crossroads in total. Upon entering the village, they encountered two crossroads, and at each corner, another one appeared.

They continued their journey to the other side of the village, enjoying the splendid views of miles of rolling green hills dotted with low-lying stone walls and ancient castles.

"We have more ancient castles in our county than any other county in Ireland," Patrick said proudly.

CHAPTER 13

The Local Pub

After finishing their lunch, Patrick suggested to Erich that they go to the pub.

"A great place to meet the locals," Patrick said.

"Mind you, I could do with a pint of stout," he added.

"I hope they can understand my thick German accent," Erich said with a chuckle.

"Ah sure, I think you'll have just as hard a time understanding their thick Irish accent," Patrick replied.

Margaret shot a disapproving glance at Patrick.

"Make sure you're back for supper by 6:00 pm," she said, shaking her head.

Margaret knew all too well that this was not going to happen!

As Erich entered the pub, he bumped his head on the door frame.

"Watch your head, young man," Patrick said.

"The problem with these old buildings is that the doorways are designed for someone under six feet tall," he added.

The small, dimly lit pub offered a warm, cozy atmosphere. It was nearly empty, save for two men at the bar with their pints of stout, smoking pipes and chatting with the barman. When Patrick and Erich entered, the men turned their attention to them, nodding with curiosity, eager to learn more about the stranger accompanying Patrick.

"This is my grandnephew Erich from Germany," he told the men.

"Thomas O'Shea, but you can call me Tommy," he said, shaking Erich's hand.

"Iain O'Connor. Nice to meet you, Erich."

'Tis a long way from your neck of the woods, young man. What brings you here?" Iain asked.

All three men gazed curiously at Erich.

Just as Erich was about to answer their question, Patrick interrupted.

"He will be helping Margaret and me on the farm. God willing, we could use an extra pair of hands," he said.

"Sure, I understand what you mean; it's hard to find good farm hands these days," Tommy acknowledged.

The other two men nodded in agreement.

"Oh sure, they're leaving in droves to head to England for a better life. My youngest son took off last summer, and we didn't see it coming," Iain exclaimed.

"We would be lucky if he gets to come home for Christmas, God willing," he added as an afterthought.

The barman, who also owned the pub, introduced himself.

"Ah, where are my manners, Sean O'Dea."

"So, how long are you planning to stay, Erich?" he asked.

Erich suddenly felt caught off guard and had to think quickly.

"Oh, however long Patrick needs me," he said, patting his granduncle on the back.

"Well, he's lucky to have you! I could use an extra pair of hands," Tommy said.

Erich realized that he needed to be careful not to reveal too much about himself, especially in a close-knit community like this where people thrived on gossip!

Patrick guided Erich away from the group and into a cozy corner for some privacy. The snug, as it was called, could comfortably accommodate two to four people; more than that and it would be a tight fit. The pub featured four snug areas, each with a small round table, a bench, and two stools.

"My favorite spot. It's also a great spot for women to enjoy their drinks. Mind you, it's not a woman's place to be seen in the pub," Patrick said.

Erich recognized that women's roles in Irish society were primarily confined to the home, sharply contrasting with women's roles in German society.

As the evening wore on, more people began to trickle in. For some, it was just a quick drink for the road, while others stayed until closing. Patrick and Erich struck up a conversation with a couple of farmers who were haggling over the price of a bull. Patrick was asked for his opinion on what a fair price was, and after so many pints of stout, Erich could barely see his granduncle through the thick haze of tobacco smoke.

"Ah Jesus, it's 9 o'clock. Margaret is going to kill me," Patrick said.

They had been at the pub since 4 pm; it was time to get on their bikes and head home!

Margaret was furious with Patrick and Erich for arriving drunk well past dinner time. Patrick, who could barely stand on his own two feet, leaned against Erich for support and sang to his heart's content. Erich also looked worse for wear; he didn't say much but wore a sheepish grin. Margaret stood with her hands on her hips, lips tightly pursed, glaring at Patrick, who appeared oblivious. She was nearly at boiling point, feeling as if she could explode, but decided it was best not to create a scene in front of Erich - one she might regret later. Margaret believed it was better to wait until morning to talk with Patrick.

"Well, I'll head to bed then; supper has gone cold. You'd better get on with it and make sure you clean up after yourselves," she said rather curtly.

"I don't want to see a mess in the morning!" She added.

"Ah, Jesus, women, don't give me such a hard time. How often do we have someone special visiting us?" Patrick slurred.

Margaret was mortified and angry with Patrick for being in such a drunken state.

"Mary, merciful God, what was he thinking? Such behavior - how embarrassing in front of her grandson! She thought to herself.

Margaret knew very well that this was Patrick's weakness; he was a little bit too fond of the drink. She had to remind herself that Patrick had his good qualities - he worked hard, managed the farm well, they never went without, and there was always food on the table. She was also grateful that Patrick had always been there for her, especially when she was widowed and pregnant at 22. If it hadn't been for him, she would have ended up in the poorhouse. She reflected on how lucky and grateful she was for what she had and couldn't have been happier to have her grandson here. Yet, this was no excuse.

CHAPTER 14

Life on the Farm

To Erich, life in Ireland seemed much simpler than in Berlin. For one thing, the living conditions at the farmhouse were rather basic. Erich was surprised to learn that Margaret and Patrick had no electricity. He was astonished to learn that a hydroelectric plant in the nearby county had been completed in 1929, yet many people still lacked electricity in their homes.

"Can you believe it? It's 1938, and most of us still don't have electricity!" Patrick said, shrugging his shoulders.

"Even in cities and towns, not everyone has electricity in their homes. Many of us still rely on the old oil lamps. I suppose we must make do!" he added.

Erich was also surprised that the farmhouse lacked a toilet or bathroom. Instead, Margaret and Patrick had to make do with a shed at the back of the house that served as an outdoor toilet, requiring manual flushing with a bucket of water. At night, a chamber pot under the bed served as a toilet. As for bathing, each bedroom had a large porcelain jug and a matching wash basin on a stand. Even though he found it somewhat cumbersome, the breathtaking views of rolling green hills from his bedroom window made it all worthwhile. He felt completely at home.

"You've taken to it like a duck to water," Patrick said.

Patrick treated Erich as if he were his son, and Margaret adored him.

"Oh, you look so much like your mother! If only she could see you now," she gushed.

Then the sobbing would begin.

For Erich, returning to the farm revived both his joyful childhood memories and the painful reminder of losing his parents. However, it didn't take long for him to adapt to life on the farm. Erich reveled in the deafening silence of the night, occasionally interrupted by the creaking of the old house, leaving one to imagine old ghosts roaming in the dead of night. He also loved waking up at the crack of dawn to the familiar sounds of farm life coming alive with the rooster's "cock-a-doodle-doo," the birds chirping in the trees, the cows mooing, eager to be milked and fed, and the pigs oinking, all signaling the start of a new day. With the symphony of morning animal sounds, it was time for Margaret and Patrick to rise and prepare for their morning chores. As for Erich, it was time to get out of bed!

The first chore of the day involved milking and feeding the cows, feeding the pigs, and caring for the horses. Erich took on the task of feeding the horses and cleaning the stable, while Patrick handled the cows and Margaret managed the pigs. After Margaret finished with the pigs, her next task was to prepare breakfast and pack lunch for

Patrick and Erich to take with them for their day's work in the fields. They had plenty of work that kept them busy from dawn until dusk.

Erich observed that the working conditions on the farm were challenging and physically demanding; regardless of the weather - rain or shine - work still had to be done. When he first arrived at the farm, he didn't possess the typical hands of a farmer - those that are rough and calloused. Rather, his hands were soft and well-manicured - those of a city dweller, an office worker. As for Erich's physical condition, thanks to his years of rigorous training in the German military, he was in great shape.

Erich also observed that Margaret and Patrick were humble and hardy people who were grateful for what little they had. They were pretty much self-sufficient in their way of life. Their primary source of income came from the milk and butter they produced and sold to neighbors and nearby villages. They had a neighboring farmer mill their wheat and either sold the flour they received or used it for bartering with their neighbors; any surplus was set aside for baking their bread. When there was an urgent need for money, Patrick would sell one or two cows at the weekly farmers' market. This involved leading the cows on a five-mile trek to the town center, where farmers gathered to sell their livestock. Erich observed that they never had to worry about having enough food on the table, and nothing went to waste.

Margaret maintained a garden that provided them with potatoes, carrots, parsnips, and cabbage. They also had an ample supply of meat. Once or twice a year, Patrick would bring a fattened pig to the local butcher, who would turn it into sausages, pork chops, ham, and black and white puddings. This meat supply would sustain them for about six months, providing sufficient protein for their daily meals. They also raised chickens that roamed freely in their backyard, ensuring a steady supply of fresh eggs and meat. Although Margaret secured the chickens at night, the foxes often succeeded in getting into the coop, escaping with a distressed chicken in their mouths and leaving behind a trail of blood and feathers.

"Those cunning, sneaky foxes are a bloody nuisance," Margaret said shaking her head in frustration.

"Before you know it, they've come and gone," she exclaimed.

To Erich, Margaret was an amazing cook. Her straightforward cooking method impressed him; it involved a large black cast-iron pot suspended from an iron rod above an open fireplace. Margaret placed hot coals on the pot lid to ensure the food cooked evenly. Every Sunday, she roasted a chicken on a spit over the fireplace. Occasionally, she prepared rabbit stew, trading with a friend or neighbor who would provide a rabbit in exchange for butter and eggs.

Erich noticed that Margaret and Patrick liked having friends and neighbors visit unexpectedly in the evenings to say hello. Some would visit to play cards, hold music sessions, and share ghost stories late into the night. Others would gather around the fire, warming their cold hands and feet while discussing the weather.

"Ah Jesus, it's shockingly cold out there, that wind would cut you in two," Paddy shared.

"It rained cats and dogs all night, sure Jesus I didn't get a wink of sleep!" Sean chimed in.

Erich Observed that Patrick was a good listener. People respected him and often sought his advice on farming or personal matters over a glass or two of Irish whiskey. Margaret would sit in the corner by the fireplace, rocking in her chair and knitting while chatting about the weather and local gossip. Occasionally, Patrick would take out his violin and start playing, encouraging his guests to join in and sing along. Some of the songs were in Gaelic, with Margaret translating for Erich.

As the night wore on, the gas lamps dimmed, casting eerie shadows across the room and creating the perfect atmosphere for ghost stories. When conversation ran dry, they sat in silence, lost in deep thought, gazing into the depths of the fire, captivated by the dancing, flickering flames before them. Erich felt the warmth of the fire, accompanied by the crackling and hissing of the wood, luring him into a drowsy state. Once everyone had left, it was time for bed, but Erich's imagination got the better of him. His mind wandered to the ghost stories that had just been shared, making it difficult for him to fall asleep.

CHAPTER 15

Spring Is in the Air

Spring is in the air, and Margaret is ready for spring cleaning.

"Young man, it's best to stay out of her way; otherwise, she'll have you doing something. You won't escape, mark my words," Patrick warned Erich, giving him a nudge and a wink.

Erich felt relieved to see the days getting warmer, especially since his arrival in March when it had been raining non-stop morning, noon, and night.

"God willing, we could do with a bit of sunshine, the best tonic anyone could ask for," Margaret exclaimed.

Erich and Patrick couldn't agree more. The days were getting warmer and, for the most part, mostly sunny, occasionally interrupted by light showers.

Another sign of spring's arrival was the garden, which was in full bloom with yellow and golden daffodils. Margaret placed vases filled with these vibrant flowers around the house, and their bright yellow and golden hues lifted everyone's spirits. Additionally, Mother Nature was truly at her finest during this time of year, especially with the lambing season. The sounds of the newborn lambs echoed across the fields. While some stayed close to their mothers, others playfully bounced around, bleating to their hearts' content.

After being cooped up indoors for so long, it didn't take Erich long to shake off his winter blues. He noticed that people were spending more time outside, enjoying the fresh country air, and seemed more cheerful. Patrick also longed for the outdoors. After breakfast, they would either go for a bike ride or take a long walk. Patrick was excited because it marked the start of the hurling season and the crossroad dances.

"Ah, I love this time of year, especially with the crossroad dances starting next Sunday," Patrick said.

"Every Sunday at 5 pm, people gather at the crossroads for a dance, and it's not always in the same place - it's spread by word of mouth," he added.

"A great place to meet a young woman," Patrick remarked, nudging Erich.

At the first crossroad dance, Erich saw two musicians arrive: a boy with a fiddle and another with a concertina. Four young boys, no older than fifteen, sat on the wall, patiently waiting for the girls to show up. Eventually, a few girls arrived but stood off to the side, giggling and chatting among themselves. They soon grew bored and left, disappointing the boys, who shortly afterward dispersed.

"Sure, it's a slow start, but trust me, more people will show up next time," Patrick said.

The following Sunday, at the village crossroads, Patrick brought his fiddle and joined two young boys - one with a violin and the other with a tin whistle. This time, more people showed up.

Erich stood off to the side, observing the dancers, and then his gaze locked onto her - he couldn't take his eyes off her. Patrick followed Erich's gaze and saw that he was interested in one of the young women. Thinking Erich was taking too long to make his move, Patrick set down his fiddle, walked over, grabbed Erich by the elbow, and guided him toward the young woman.

"Now you young, fair maidens, it's wonderful of you to honor us with your presence on such a fine evening. Let me introduce you: Erich, this is Maud and Eileen. Girls, this is Erich, my grandnephew from Germany," Patrick said.

"Would you, young lady, do this old man the honor of dancing with me?" Patrick asked Eileen.

"Of course, it would be my pleasure," Eileen giggled. Patrick quickly guided Eileen onto the dance floor, leaving Erich and Maud alone. For a moment, Erich felt taken by surprise.

"That crafty old bastard has really put me on the spot," Erich's inner voice said.

"So, you're Patrick's famous grandnephew from Germany. Nice to meet you," Maud said, pulling Erich out of his reverie.

"Likewise, it's my pleasure," Erich replied.

For a brief moment, Erich felt as though time had come to a complete standstill and that they had the entire place to themselves. He suddenly realized he had been staring at her for far too long - long enough for her to find it off-putting - yet he couldn't stop gazing at her. He noticed she was tall, about five feet, eight inches, and slim in build. Her thick, curly auburn hair was loosely tucked beneath her beret, giving her a chic vibe. He also assumed she was younger than he was, probably in her early twenties, which seemed a fitting age for someone nearing twenty-seven.

They stood there silently for a moment.

"I'm sorry; I'm unfamiliar with this type of dancing. It's all new to me. Erich admitted.

"Perhaps you could show me," he said, gesturing towards the floor.

Maud led Erich onto the dance floor; her warmth and friendly demeanor put him at ease. After his unsuccessful attempts at Irish dancing, Maud quickly guided him to the stone wall, where they sat and talked for what felt like an eternity. She shared that she was an English teacher and taught in the nearby village.

"I have a boyfriend, but we've known each other since we were five, and we're more like friends than anything else," Maud shared.

Erich felt relieved when Maud revealed that she wasn't in a serious relationship, filling him with hope of getting to know her in due time. He didn't want the night to end and was disappointed when she had to leave.

"I better get going. I need to make sure my brother Ian gets home," Maud said, pointing at the boy playing the fiddle.

"He's starting a new job tomorrow at the local creamery - my boyfriend's family business," she added.

Before he knew it, she was gone, leaving him standing there, wondering if he would see her again. Erich felt his heart flutter and was reassured that they had parted on a positive note. "Maud, what a lovely name," he thought to himself.

Not long after Maud left with her brother Ian and her friend Eileen, others soon followed. Shortly after that, Patrick and Erich made their way home.

"A bit tongue-tied, aren't we? Maud has certainly caught your fancy. She's pretty, isn't she?' Patrick said.

Erich couldn't agree more - he felt lovestruck!

"You see, Maud lost her father to meningitis when she was just four. You can't imagine how difficult it was for her mother, Sheila, who was left with four young mouths to feed: Ian, who was barely out of his crib, and Maud's two older brothers, John, six, and Brian, eight. Patrick shared.

Fortunately for Sheila, her family lived nearby, and the community offered support. In the worst-case scenario, she could have ended up in a poor house, and God only knows what would have happened to the children. Just the thought of it makes me shudder," he continued.

Erich's thoughts were solely of Maud, wondering if he would see her again.

CHAPTER 16

Maud

After meeting Erich at the crossroads dance, Maud couldn't stop thinking about him, the mysterious foreigner she had just met. She considered how tall and handsome he was, standing at least six feet two inches tall and towering over her five-foot-eight-inch frame. Her friend Eileen teased her.

"Well, I'd say, if it weren't so dark, you'd be blushing from ear to ear. Sex on legs! "Where the hell did he come from? And what is he doing in our neck of the woods? Does he have friends?" Eileen teased.

"Oh, stop it, Eileen, isn't he just. I feel like I've been struck by lightning," Maud gushed.

"I hope I'll see him again!" she added.

Ian found the girls irritating, with their banter and giggling like silly schoolgirls - he had had quite enough.

"Oh, come on, you two! Can't you wait until I'm not here? I don't want to hear all that silly girl talk!" he exclaimed.

Maud linked her arm with her brother's, and they walked home in silence.

That night, Maud couldn't sleep; her thoughts were only of Erich. His German accent, deep voice, and the distinctive scar down the right side of his cheek made him even more alluring. Maud imagined Erich holding her in his arms and kissing her tenderly as she ran her fingers through his dark, wavy hair. She longed to be swept away by this handsome stranger, a foreigner stirring up feelings she had never felt before. Maud felt a strong bond between them. Was it love at first sight, or was it lust? Perhaps, she wondered a little bit of both!

Maud reminded herself that she had a boyfriend, Colin. They were childhood sweethearts who had known each other since they were five. They practically grew up together and began dating when they were seventeen. Her mother had emphasized the importance of saving one's virginity for the wedding night. The sound of her mother's voice echoed in her mind.

"Mark my words, no man wants damaged goods. Behind every good man stands a good woman," Sheila stressed.

"If only your father were here, he would offer you some advice. There's only so much I can give. God rest his soul," she added.

At 22, Maud realized that most girls her age were either getting engaged, married, or having babies. To her annoyance, her mother had recently started suggesting that she shouldn't wait too long.

"You're not getting any younger," Sheila remarked.

"You can't go wrong with Colin. He's a good man and has a decent job. He's not going to wait for you forever," she emphasized.

Maud acknowledged that Colin was a great catch; he was attractive, stable, and financially secure. Colin, the youngest of five brothers, assisted his father in operating their family creamery, which provided milk and butter to the surrounding communities, making them quite prosperous. Maud and Sheila appreciated Colin and his family for giving Ian a job. With few job opportunities available elsewhere, they worried that Ian might get up to no good.

After meeting Erich that evening, Maud began to question her relationship with Colin, and now she felt confused about her feelings for him. He was the only man she had ever dated. Most of the young men she came across were either unemployed or too fond of the drink. The decent ones were either married or had moved to England. As her friend Eileen had noted:

"There's plenty of fish in the sea, but not enough salmon."

Maud felt she wasn't ready to settle down yet and didn't see herself as a wife, let alone a mother. A strong-minded young woman, Maud wasn't shy about expressing her thoughts, especially since her two older brothers moved to England, leaving her, her widowed mother, and her brother Ian behind. With limited job opportunities in Ireland, she couldn't blame them, though she often felt the weight of responsibility on her shoulders, especially when it came to household decisions.

Her brothers, John, twenty-four, and Brian, twenty-six, joined the throngs of young Irish men and women taking the boat to England in search of a better life. They frequently wrote to their mother and sent her whatever small amount of cash they could spare. They reported that jobs were plentiful and life was good for them, always signing off: "Wished we lived closer. Hugs and kisses xxx."

Maud missed John and Brian dearly, and it broke her mother's heart not knowing when she would see them again, despite their promise to be home for Christmas. Maud recalled that soon after they left for England, she could hear her mother crying herself to sleep. As time passed, her mother gradually adjusted to the absence of her sons. Although Maud was tempted to join them, she felt it wouldn't be right to leave her mother and Ian behind, as it would feel like abandoning them. Furthermore, she loved her teaching job at the local village school.

With no male head in the Aherne household, money was somewhat tight. However, they managed to get by on Maud's earnings and Sheila's tailoring of suits and dresses, keeping their heads above water. Now that Ian will be working for Colin's family creamery, the extra money will come in handy.

CHAPTER 17

Erich – Reflection

After meeting Maud, Erich couldn't stop thinking about her. However, his feelings for her also brought back painful memories of his ex-girlfriend, Hilda. They had been together for two years, but their relationship ended abruptly. Their differing political views drove them apart, especially given the volatile political climate they lived in.

Erich realized that ending his relationship with Hilda was a hard and painful choice. He believed that she had become overly radicalized, especially regarding her hostility toward Jews. This became apparent when Erich's upstairs neighbors, a middle-aged Jewish couple named Issak and Berta Distler, had to sell their apartment and move.

"I'll be glad to see the last of those Jews. Good riddance to them," Hilda said.

At first, Erich was taken aback. The animosity in Hilda's voice was unmistakable, especially her hatred for Jewish people. Despite being in a committed relationship with her, this was the first time

Erich saw a genuinely ugly side of Hilda. In an instant, he went right off her. The thought of spending the rest of his life with her was now out of the question.

Erich felt sympathy for the Distlers, who had been good neighbors to his family for over thirty years. After his parents' tragic death, they took care of their apartment, which had been vacant for several years. Issak, a tax consultant, and Berta, a woman of leisure, were well-off. When Erich returned to his family's apartment after graduating from university, the Distlers welcomed him as if he were one of their own.

The year 1936 was a difficult year for the Distlers. At the beginning of the year, a new Nuremberg law was enacted, prohibiting Jews from working as tax consultants, and soon after, Issak found himself unemployed. This was a significant setback for them. Their means of support were taken away, just as it was for thousands of other German Jews. Around this time, Erich noticed that the Distlers started to distance themselves from him. He understood their perspective, especially considering the widespread anti-Jewish sentiment in German society, and his association with the Gestapo, said a lot. Erich couldn't imagine what they were experiencing, but he felt powerless because there was nothing he could do.

Shortly thereafter, more laws surfaced that effectively marginalized the Jewish communities within German society. The Distlers chose to leave Berlin, as remaining there would have sentenced them to a life of misery and poverty. Fortunately, they departed for America that summer after Isaak's brother in New York arranged safe passage for them. Eric visited them just before their departure, wishing them the best of luck and a safe journey.

Erich also reflected on one of the most significant events of that year: the 1936 Summer Olympic Games, held that August. As the Olympic Games drew near, there was an urgent desire to hide the signs of anti-Jewish sentiment. Erich noted that in the days leading up to and during the Summer Olympics, the streets of Berlin were cleared of anti-Jewish posters. Additionally, local newspapers toned down their anti-Jewish rhetoric. This was intended to show foreign visitors and the international media that Germany was a peaceful and tolerant nation towards the Jewish community. To further quell anti-Jewish rumors, the Third Reich allowed a Jewish athlete, Helene Mayer, a fencer, to participate in the Olympic Games. Mayer was classified as non-Aryan due to her father's Jewish heritage. Despite efforts by the United States and Europe to boycott the Olympic Games, the events proceeded as scheduled.

Nearly two years later, Erich appreciates his time in Ireland, relishing the tranquility of a laid-back place where he feels that world news is largely censored. His thoughts drifted back to Maud Aherne; he had never felt this way about anyone - true love at first sight. Yet, his conscience urged him not to get involved, as someone would inevitably be hurt. After all, he was on a mission for the Third Reich, waiting for orders, though he didn't know when they would come.

CHAPTER 18

Crossing Paths Again

It didn't take long for Erich and Maud to cross paths again; it was the following Sunday at church when he saw her. He spotted her sitting a few pews down and observed the light streaming through the window, capturing the golden tones of her auburn hair. Erich sat there counting the minutes away, not listening to a word the priest said; it felt like an eternity.

"Mass has ended, go in peace," the priest said.

Erich felt his heart pounding. He was excited to see Maud again, but with her boyfriend, Colin, beside her, he felt apprehensive. However, from what he learned from Maud, her relationship with Colin appeared more like that of good friends.

He remembered that evening when they first met at the Crossroads dance, and after they went their separate ways, he confided in Patrick that he wished to see her again.

"Ah, sure, I've known Colin since he was a baby - he's a good lad," Patrick said, shaking Erich out of his reverie.

"Mind you, I think Maud has taken a liking to you. If you want to see her again, she'll be at the 11 o'clock mass on Sunday," Patrick added.

Be careful, though; I don't think Colin will take too kindly to a stranger, a foreigner such as yourself, taking an interest in his girl-friend," he cautioned.

Erich assured Patrick that he would be discreet!

After the church service, Erich, Margaret, Patrick, Maud, Colin, Ian, and Sheila stood by the church gates exchanging some pleasantries.

"It's a fine morning, let's hope the rain stays off," Margaret said.

Everyone nodded in agreement. Ian soon grew tired of being around adults. He excused himself and hurried off down the road to join his friends. Margaret and Sheila soon got into a conversation about the local gossip. Patrick and Colin became engrossed in con-versation about the upcoming hurling match. Meanwhile, Maud and Erich stood to the side, caught up in a moment of silence.

Erich found it enduring when Maud's cheeks flushed a deep shade of red. Maud felt her heart skip a beat and could feel her cheeks burn-ing. She was relieved that Colin was too engrossed in conversation with Patrick to notice the chemistry between her and Erich.

"It's nice to see you again," Erich said, shaking Maud out of her reverie.

"You too," Maud replied.

"And how are you settling into Irish life? I am sure it's a big change from Berlin" she said.

"Yes, it's a big change," he replied.

Then he paused momentarily.

"One thing for sure, I don't miss the hustle and bustle of city life," he exclaimed.

Erich welcomed the change, the peace and quiet, and the slow pace of country life. He felt safe and was glad to distance himself from the political turmoil he had left behind. For a brief moment, Erich felt as if it were just the two of them until Patrick's hand rested on his right shoulder, pulling him back to reality.

"Is that the time already? Can you believe it? It's already forty minutes past the hour," Patrick exclaimed, glancing at his watch and running his fingers through his thick, unruly gray hair.

Erich noticed that his granduncle had a habit of doing this, especially when he felt a sense of urgency or had something on his mind.

Colin joined Maud by her side and placed his arm around her shoulders.

"Well, we best be off, love; we have a hurling match at three. I'll catch up with you later," Colin said, giving Maud a quick peck on the cheek.

"Ah, sure, there's no doubt about it; we have the best goalie here, the best all around," Patrick declared, giving Colin a pat on the back.

Erich thought this was perfect timing to have some time alone with Maud.

"I think I'll hang back for a bit," Erich said to Patrick and Margaret.

Soon after, Margaret, Patrick, and Colin rushed off, leaving Erich, Maud, and Sheila by the church gates. Maud observed that

Colin's presence earlier didn't seem to have deterred Erich, and she was aware that his feelings for her were quite mutual.

"Would you like to join me?" Erich asked Maud.

Before Maud could answer, Erich turned his attention to her mother.

"I hope that is ok with you, Mrs. Ahern," Erich asked Sheila.

Maud was pleasantly surprised by Erich's politeness in asking her mother for permission to walk with her. She suddenly felt giddy with excitement.

"Why yes. It's a lovely day! Let's make the most of it while it's sunny," Maud replied before her mother could respond to Erich.

For a brief moment, Erich, Maud, and Sheila found themselves in an awkward silence.

"Well, Maud, don't forget. I'm putting on a roast for 5:00 p.m., and Colin will be joining us," Sheila said, then she walked away.

Erich sensed that Maud's mother was bothered by her daughter taking off with him, a total stranger and a foreigner. He felt that perhaps one day he would have the chance to visit the Ahern's household and properly introduce himself. Erich was beside himself with having Maud all to himself.

CHAPTER 19

The Abbey

Erich and Maud walked toward the Abbey. As they drew closer, they were greeted by black and white cows grazing near the entrance gate, creating an idyllic scene against the backdrop of the Abbey. The cows paused briefly and curiously stared at Erich and Maud. Erich felt hesitant as he spotted a bullock, giving the impression that it could charge at them at any moment. Noticing his hesitance, Maud stepped forward.

"Shoo, shoo, shoo, shoo," she said, clapping her hands.

The cows quickly dispersed, clearing the pathway to the entrance.

"For a moment, I thought we would have to run for it," Erich said, laughing.

They quietly wandered through the Abbey grounds, a burial ground for those who departed in recent times intermingled with those long gone. They followed the narrow pathway leading them from one tombstone to the next. Erich observed the ancient tombstones of those who had long passed; their identities, once etched in stone, now faded by the passage of time. Some headstones had elaborate Celtic designs, while others were plain and simple - a reflection of one's social status in their lifetime. Maud told Erich that only those who have lived in the village for many generations could be buried here, alongside the clansmen and their families from the past. She guided Erich to her father's resting place. A large Celtic cross towered over two graves, with the names of those who departed etched in stone.

"Two generations of my father's family are buried here. My father died when I was very young, too young to remember him," Maud said.

Erich observed Maud's voice quivered, almost to the point of tears. He confided in her that he had lost both of his parents in a tragic accident when he was ten years old.

"So sorry for your loss. It's bad enough losing one parent at such a young age, but to lose both; I can't imagine," Maud said sympathetically.

Maud sensed that Erich didn't want to talk about it. They stood silently, lost in their thoughts, reflecting on their lost loved ones. For Erich, talking about his parents' death was painful. For years, he had pushed it to the back of his mind, and now, as he stood at the burial site with Maud, all those painful memories came flooding back.

As they climbed the steps of the Abbey, Erich was captivated by the breathtaking sight that unfolded before him. At the far end of the Abbey, sunlight streamed through the tall, arched, windowless openings, casting beams of light across a spacious room. The sunlight intertwined with dark shadows highlighted the room's vastness with its ancient high stone walls devoid of its roof. Under the open sky, the roofless room was flooded with more light, drawing Erich's attention to the ancient altar beneath the large arched windows, indicating that this was once a place of worship. Erich felt a sudden calmness wash over him. He felt the sight before him was a testament to its historical past, a place of devotion and a final resting place for the dearly departed.

As they stepped into the vast, open space, Erich observed the large, ancient burial stones beneath their feet, some more elaborate than others. The entire room was filled with burial stones, with no clear pathway to avoid stepping on them. The carvings and inscriptions have long faded due to exposure to the elements and countless footsteps over the centuries.

"Mostly bishops, monks, and prominent members of the Franciscan order are buried here," Maud said.

Maud motioned for Erich to follow her to the corner of the room, where a tomb with its heavy stone slab was embedded in the wall. Above it, a 17th-century medieval crucifix stood.

"This 17th-century crucifix serves as a reminder of the Cromwellian era when Cromwell's forces killed Franciscan monks and destroyed Abbeys throughout Ireland," Maud exclaimed.

"I can't imagine what they must have gone through – such desecration of their sacred ground - and what faith awaited them," she added.

As they reached the end of the room, they found themselves in the cloister, where shafts of sunlight mingled with dark shadows streaming through the stone arches that framed the courtyard. The light beams illuminated a space surrounded by darkness, with large, ancient burial stones lining the pathway beneath their feet.

Erich felt its peacefulness, a quiet haven with the allure of its haunted past. He envisioned the clansmen of its time and later the bishops, Franciscan monks, and priests. They stood in silence, absorbing an atmosphere that truly felt haunted by the spirits of the past.

"Whenever I need some space, this is where I lose myself in deep thought," Maud said, shaking Erich out of his reverie.

"As a child, I found this place terrifying, especially with all the dead buried here. My grandfather used to say, 'The dead can't harm the living. You have nothing to be afraid of, my child,'" Maud remarked, imitating her grandfather's voice.

They continued exploring the cloister, wandering in and out of the adjacent rooms. Maud noted every room - the chapter room, the kitchen, the refectory, and the dormitory. Each room felt cold, dark, and damp, creating an eerie atmosphere. Erich observed the small and large headstones in the far corners of each room; their inscriptions faded with the passage of time.

Maud pointed out to Erich the ornate resting place of the clansmen, most notably the O'Briens and the MacNamara Chieftains. Despite the Abbey's tragic past and the souls long buried within its structures, the place had a haunting and spiritual beauty.

Just off the cloister, Erich and Maud carefully ascended the narrow, dark stairwell to the second floor. Just as Maud was about to step into the open space, a sudden glare of sunlight temporarily blinded her, causing her to lose her footing and stumble forward. As she fell, Erich swiftly grabbed her hand and pulled her back, letting her fall into his arms. For a brief moment, they stood close together. Erich noticed Maud's cheeks flush a deep red, making this beautiful woman in his arms even more alluring. He wanted to kiss her but thought otherwise, as this was not the right time, so he let her go. They stood awkwardly for a moment, both at a loss for words. Maud was the first to break the silence, her voice with a slight stutter:

"This place is said to be haunted by Donough Beg O'Brian, hung from that steeple in the late 16th century," Maud said, pointing toward the steeple they were about to climb.

"Some say his lost soul still wanders the dark corridors of the Abbey, and his eerie cries can be heard echoing throughout. Yet, is it only the wind whistling through the vast expanse of the Abbey that gets the better of one's imagination?" Maud explained.

Erich and Maud ascended a short flight of steps, which led them onto a narrow walkway. They cautiously walked along the narrow walkway until they reached a spiral staircase that led them up to the tower. Upon reaching the tower, they were met with splendid views of the surrounding countryside. Erich was beside himself; he savored the moment, taking it all in. Alone with a beautiful woman and surrounded by breathtaking views, he couldn't ask for anything more. The warmth from the sun was a welcome relief from the cold, dark, and damp depths below. It was a perfect day.

"To think of it, when we were kids, we used to walk along that narrow wall," Maud said, pointing at the wall below.

"Just one misstep, a broken neck, and worse, death - just the thought of it! Well, as a kid, you don't think about the dangers," she continued.

"The things we did as kids," Erich chuckled.

They stood quietly for a moment, gazing at each other. Maud looked down at her watch and let out a sigh.

"I best be getting home, or my mum will wonder why we're taking so long. Knowing her, I won't hear the end of it," she said.

"Well, I don't want to keep a lady waiting after you," Erich replied.

Erich and Maud made their way slowly down the stairs, leading them back into the depths of the cold, dark corridors below. Their imagination got the better of them - they could almost hear O'Brian's lost soul wandering the dark corridors, crying out in agony. It was time to go. They were glad to leave behind the cold, dark dampness of the Abbey and its ghosts of the past.

Erich walked Maud back to her house, and as they said their goodbyes, their eyes locked on each other for a moment.

"I'm sure our paths will cross again," Erich said.

"In a small place like this, I'm sure we will," Maud chuckled.

Erich hesitated for a moment, considering what to say next.

"Well, I bid you farewell until we meet again," he said.

As Erich walked away, he glanced back and saw Maud still standing in the doorway, her hand resting on the doorframe, watching him leave. Their eyes locked onto each other once more, but their moment was interrupted by Sheila.

"Is that you, Maud," Sheila called out, coming to the door.

With a smile and a wave, Erich turned on his heels and headed back to Margaret and Patrick's house with a skip in his step. He felt confident they would cross paths again. Erich believed that love was truly in the air!

CHAPTER 20

Sunday Dinner

After their Sunday afternoon walk in the Abbey, Maud couldn't stop thinking about Erich; her head was in the clouds. Her mother noticed that ever since her daughter came home, her mind had been a thousand miles away, clearly preoccupied with this foreign man she barely knew.

Colin arrived for dinner at the Ahern's household shortly after 5:00 pm and apologized for being late because the hurling match had lasted longer than expected. When he found out that Maud had spent the afternoon with Erich at the Abbey, he didn't like it. Maud could sense his silent treatment at the table and had had enough. She couldn't take it any longer and confronted him.

"Since you were off playing hurling with Patrick, you didn't expect me to waste a beautiful Sunday afternoon waiting for you," Maud said.

Maud felt her anger rise when Colin didn't respond.

"Besides, Erich asked me, what could I say? He's not a total stranger, and I didn't want to seem rude," Maud said angrily.

"You don't own me, Colin. You are not my husband!" she continued.

A tense silence fell over the table to the point where you could almost hear a pin drop. Colin was speechless, and Sheila was mortified. Ian quickly finished his dinner, made his excuses, and left the table. Suddenly, the atmosphere felt uncomfortable; the silence was deafening.

"Love, I'm sorry. I didn't mean what I just said," Maud said, gently placing her hand over Colin's.

"It's okay. I was out of line. You're right; you're not my wife. I think I best be going; it's getting late, and I have an early start in the morning," Colin replied.

Colin thanked Sheila for the delicious dinner and headed toward the hallway. Sheila gestured for her daughter to follow.

Maud followed him to the door, sensing he was visibly upset and angry with her.

"I'll catch up with you later in the week," Colin said, giving Maud a quick kiss on the cheek.

Maud watched Colin walk away, his shoulders hunched, and not once did he look back at her. She regretted how they parted ways but didn't regret her outburst; perhaps she felt she could have been more diplomatic. Regardless, she didn't believe things would have turned out differently; Colin would still be angry with her, and there was no doubt he was jealous of Erich due to his competitiveness. She felt bad, but at the same time, after meeting Erich, she had gained a different perspective on her relationship with Colin.

When Maud returned to the room, Sheila looked concerned and

unhappy with her daughter's behavior, prompting her to lecture her.

"By the way, this Erich fellow, he's a fine-looking young man and at least a few years older than you. After all, he is a foreigner, and you know absolutely nothing about him," Sheila exclaimed.

Maud didn't take too kindly to her mother's lecture.

"Mum, I am a grown woman. Stop treating me like a child. He's almost 27 - five years older than me and no stranger to these parts. After all, he's Margaret's grandson and spent most of his childhood summers here," Maud said curtly.

"What about Colin? You can't keep him hanging on. He is not going to wait around for you forever, you know," Sheila retorted.

"And what about you, mum? Maud fired back.

"Look, Mum, Dad's been gone for many years; isn't it about time you had someone to take care of you?" Maud said more sympathetically.

"This is not about me, young lady; don't change the subject! Colin worships the ground you walk on, and you know he would marry you in a heartbeat," Sheila exclaimed.

"I worry about you, my love. I only want what's best for you. Besides this Erich fellow, you don't know how long he will be here for. He could break your heart and bugger off back to Berlin tomorrow,' Sheila continued.

Maud knew her mother was right; she knew nothing about Erich, his intentions, or how long he would be in Ireland for. There was a risk he could break her heart and vanish from her life entirely. Yet, she felt willing to take that chance. What if? If she doesn't take it, she might regret it for the rest of her life. Even though she had only met him recently, Maud felt an instant attraction to Erich, and there was undeniable chemistry between them.

She replayed the scene in her mind from their time at the Abbey. When they reached the second level, she tripped on the last step, sending her flying forward, and Erich broke her fall. It all happened so quickly; she found herself in his arms. His eyes locked onto hers, and she was certain he wanted to kiss her in that moment but thought better of it. She replayed that moment over and over in her mind, feeling a sudden wave of warmth fill her chest. Perhaps she was imagining it, but she sensed that something almost happened between them. Or maybe Erich was caught off guard and was just being the perfect gentleman. If anything were to happen between them in the future, it would be a risk worth taking.

CHAPTER 21

The Breakup

Since they parted ways that Sunday on not such a great note, Colin noticed that things between him and Maud were not good. He blamed Erich for waltzing into their lives and trying to steal his girlfriend away. Despite Maud's reassurances that nothing had happened between them, Colin wasn't convinced. He feared losing her to this foreigner, and he noticed she became easily irritated whenever he brought up the subject. One day, they ran into Erich and Patrick in town. They exchanged some pleasantries with each other, and then the penny dropped!

Colin noticed how Erich looked at Maud, his gaze intimate, and her cheeks flushed a deep red in response! There was no denying it; there was a mutual attraction between the two, and the sickening part was that Maud giggled like a silly schoolgirl. Colin suddenly felt insecure and began to see Erich as a threat, competing for the woman he loved. This only reinforced his suspicion that Erich was interested in his girlfriend. He felt angry but decided to keep his feelings to himself. He didn't want to give Erich the satisfaction of coming across as the jealous, possessive boyfriend, nor did he want to lose Maud! After all, Maud was a beautiful and strong-minded woman; any man would be lucky to have her; he was the envy of the village.

"Who does this fucking kraut think he is, waltzing in here like he owns the place! What, with that thick German accent, I would love to wipe that fucking smile off his face!" Colin thought to himself.

Colin noticed a certain air about Erich. He seemed a well-refined man, good-looking, charismatic, and with impeccable manners.

"For all you know, he could have a wife back home," he thought to himself.

Colin knew one thing about Maud: her face was easily readable, and she wasn't good at hiding things. He let it slide for a few days until one night, after walking her home from the pub, he came right out and said it.

"Is there anything going on between you two?" Colin exclaimed.

"What are you talking about?" Maud responded.

"Come on, Maud; you know who I mean. The other day in town, I noticed how you looked at him, and he looked at you. There's no denying it, you like him," Colin said angrily.

Colin could have kicked himself for letting his temper get the better of him. He was all too aware that he was coming across as the jealous, possessive boyfriend. He couldn't help it; he didn't want to lose her. After all, she was the only girlfriend he ever had. They practically grew up together since childhood!

"No, Colin, nothing happened between Erich and me. Truth be told, I want it to happen," Maud replied bluntly.

"I'm sorry, Colin. I didn't mean to be so blunt, but there you have it. That's how I feel. I think we shouldn't see each other for a while. I'm sorry, but there's no other way," Maud continued.

Colin was speechless. He couldn't believe Maud had just broken up with him; he had never seen this coming. Maud assured him that Erich had nothing to do with it and reminded him that neither of them had ever been with anyone else.

"I think it's time we take a break! I swear to you on my father's grave, nothing has happened between Erich and me," Maud said reassuringly to Colin.

Colin struggled to accept that Maud, the love of his life, had just broken up with him. He couldn't imagine life without her, as he worshipped the very ground she walked on! He thought they had a future together, and that she would be the mother of his children. All it took was a stranger to waltz into town and ruin it for them.

"We've grown apart. This is something I have felt for some time. It has taken someone like Erich for me to realize that," Maud said.

Colin felt numb and reflected on how cruel Maud's words sounded, especially the part where she said she was very fond of him. In other words, she was not in love with him, nor had she ever been, for that matter.

"Stop! Just stop! I've heard enough! Colin exclaimed.

He turned and walked away, leaving her at the front doorstep without a goodbye.

"Colin, please, I'm sorry, but that's just how it is," Maud called after him.

His entire world had just been turned upside down! He had just lost the love of his life, the one he thought he had a future with. And who was to blame for this was Erich.

.

CHAPTER 22

Gathering of the Hay

From dawn until dusk, Patrick, Margaret, and Erich were out in the fields, busy cutting and gathering hay. Erich noticed that Patrick and Margaret were both excited and nervous, as it was that busy time of year again; the haymaking season had just begun. Erich observed that many men from the village were willing to lend Patrick a hand by arriving with their pitchforks and rakes, ready for a long day's work. Later in the day, their children and friends would arrive, all too eager to gather the hay and, for the younger ones, play hide-and-seek among the haystacks.

With the haymaking season in full swing, Erich was exhausted at the end of the day. But upon hearing the news of Maud and Colin's breakup, he felt it was time to ask her out. From the moment he saw her, he couldn't stop thinking about her and that Sunday at the Abbey; their time alone only reinforced Erich's feelings for her. He would lay awake at night, longing for her to be in his arms. Erich felt excited when Margaret announced that Maud and her mother would join them in the morning to help gather the hay.

Margaret observed her grandson's face light up when she announced that Maud and her mother would join them in the morning. Even when Erich offered to help clean up after dinner that night, she wouldn't hear of it.

"Off to bed with you now, my love. You have an early start tomorrow. I'll get things done quicker here without you under my feet," Margaret said.

That night, Erich didn't sleep a wink - all night, he couldn't stop thinking about Maud. In the morning, he jumped out of bed, excited to see her again.

By 7 am, Patrick and Erich were already in the field cutting hay. Shortly after, Maud and Sheila arrived at the farmhouse, eager to help Margaret prepare refreshments and food for the workers. The women found the farmhouse to be warm and welcoming. On entering, they were hit by the lingering smell of freshly baked bread that Margaret had baked earlier that morning. With the arrival of Maud and Sheila, the kitchen buzzed with laughter and excitement for the day's event ahead. Margaret assigned tasks to the women: Maud beat the eggs, and Sheila rolled the dough for the apple pies while Margaret busied herself boiling water for tea. Once the water boiled, she poured it into four large teapots with black tea and let it steep for a stronger brew. Once ready, she transferred the tea into four large flasks and added milk and sugar.

"The lads must be famished by now. We'd best head up to them soon, or there'll be a riot," Margaret chuckled.

Shortly before 10 a.m., Margaret, Maud, and Sheila headed out to the fields with their baskets of baked goods and flasks of tea.

It was a beautiful sunny day with little cloud cover and a slight chill in the air.

"What a glorious day! I hope it stays like this. Lord Jesus, we need the good dry weather," Margaret said, shielding her eyes from the sun with her hand.

As Maud approached the workers, she quickly noticed Erich standing on the hill with his back to her, leaning on his pitchfork and using his handkerchief to wipe the sweat from his face and the back of his neck. Maud observed how tall and lean he was, with a slim waist and broad shoulders. She stood there for a moment, absorbing his presence. Erich turned around, sensing that someone was watching him, and saw Maud. He gave her a big smile and waved, beckoning for her to come closer. As she approached him, a sudden wave of shyness came over her, and she could feel her cheeks burning. She noticed his shirt sleeves rolled up above his elbows, highlighting his well-defined forearms, and with a few buttons undone, revealing a glimpse of dark chest hair. Maud thought about how handsome Erich was and felt her heart flutter slightly. She could feel her cheeks burning even more. She knew she must be red as a beetroot and suddenly felt tongue-tied.

Erich was excited to see Maud and noted how lovely she looked. She wore a pair of dark blue denim dungarees with a thick belt that accentuated her slim waist and ample bosom. The blue blouse she wore underneath accentuated the color of her deep blue eyes.

Erich observed the odd curl escaping the confined space of her green scarf. He was tempted to reach out and tuck it away but thought otherwise. He noticed the sunlight reflecting off her loose curls, capturing the golden-reddish hues of her hair. They stood there momentarily, looking at one another, until Patrick interrupted them.

"We're making great progress today. Let's hope this dry spell continues," Patrick said, chewing on a blade of grass.

"Come along, lads, you must be hungry," Margaret called out.

The workers welcomed the break. Putting down their rakes and pitchforks, they gathered around the women taking what they were given; they were famished. They savored the thick slices of bread slathered with butter, homemade jam, and a slice of apple pie accompanied by a cup of hot, milky tea. Once they finished eating, some sat around laughing and talking about the day's events while others lay flat on their backs, basking in the warmth of the summer sun.

Patrick and Erich grabbed their pitchforks and returned to work, and soon the others joined them. They stacked the hay into piles, one on top of another, with some reaching seven to eight feet high. For the younger children, the highlight of their day was attempting to climb onto the haystacks, but the bigger ones proved too difficult. At the end of the workday, the men secured the haystacks by covering them with tarps and adding ropes weighted down by heavy stones.

"This will certainly keep them secure. If it rains during the night or in the coming days, we're prepared," Patrick said reassuringly.

Patrick thanked the workers for their help and invited them to stop by the farmhouse later for a drink. He also encouraged anyone with musical instruments to bring them along.

"Well, I'd best be off home to freshen up. I'll see you later and bring the lad along with his fiddle," Sheila offered.

"That would be great. We look forward to it," Patrick responded.

Sheila left while Maud stayed behind to help Margaret carry the empty baskets and flasks back to the house.

Upon arriving at the farmhouse, Margaret and Maud were greeted by two horses, their heads peeking from the stable's half door, neighing excitedly at their owners' return.

"Hello, beautiful. It's nice to meet you," Maud said, gently stroking the smaller horse's head.

Patrick soon joined Maud by her side.

"This one is a little shy; her name is Beauty," Patrick said.

"For sure, she's some speed in her. She's come in second at the point-to-point races," he added proudly.

The horse lowered her head to the sound of her name, allowing Maud to stroke her even more. Maud observed the other horse, a large and sturdy animal whose chestnut coat resembled Beauty's, except for a few white spots. But when she reached out to stroke its head, the horse pulled back, tilted its head, and snorted. The horse looked nervous, as if it could bolt at any moment.

"Ah, this is Beast, he's a bit feisty. You'd think he's possessed by the devil," Patrick cautioned.

He senses your nervousness; you need to show him who's boss," Patrick continued.

He handed Maud an apple and told her to keep her palm open so the horse could take it.

"If he bites you, I'll kick his ass from here to Timbuktu," Patrick said with a wink and a laugh.

"Young lady, have you ever ridden on a horse?" Patrick asked more seriously

"Yes, "Small ponies, if they count," Maud giggled.

"I'll tell you what, as a thank you for your help today, I'll have Erich take you out for a ride on Beauty," Patrick offered.

Patrick noticed Maud blushing at the mere mention of his grand-nephew's name. Just then, Erich joined them.

"Speaking of the devil, your ears must have been burning; we were just talking about you," Patrick said, clapping Erich gently on the back.

"Since Maud has taken to Beauty, I've offered to let her take her for a ride. Maybe you could give her a refresher riding course," Patrick suggested.

You could use a day off, young man," He added as an afterthought.

"It would be an honor. First, we need to get you acquainted with her. If all goes well, we will take you out and about. How about tomorrow at 9 am?" Erich asked Maud.

"Yes, that sounds lovely," Maud replied.

CHAPTER 23

First Outing

By the time Maud arrived, Erich had already fed and harnessed the horses and was ready for their outing. She noticed that Erich had a special way with the horses, particularly with Beast, who tended to be nervous, but under Erich's care, he remained calm. Erich gently patted Beast's side and spoke soothingly to him.

"That's a good boy," Erich said.

"When it comes to horses, you need to show them who's in control; otherwise, they can sense your nervousness," he said, motioning for Maud to come closer.

Erich thought it was important for Maud to familiarize herself with Beauty, the horse she was about to mount. He took a crab apple from his pocket and placed it in the palm of her hand. Beauty quickly snapped it up and crunched away as if savoring every bite. Maud gently stroked the horse's head.

"Hello, Beauty. This is my first riding lesson, so please be gentle with me," Maud said, stroking the horse's head.

"First, we must ensure the saddle is tight and secure before you get on. We don't want you falling off, now do we?" Erich said with a wink and a reassuring smile.

"Ready for your first lesson?" he asked.

At first, Maud felt nervous, but with Erich by her side, she quickly felt at ease. She reassured herself that Erich knew what he was doing and that she was in safe hands. Maud observed the dark clouds gathering on the horizon, signaling a chance of rain.

During breakfast, Margaret hinted to Erich that there might be a slight chance of rain later.

"With Irish weather, we can have five seasons in one day," Margaret exclaimed, just as Patrick had mentioned to Erich during their first outing.

Margaret gave Erich raincoats for him and Maud and a light snack to take with them. Erich heeded her advice and thought the sooner they got going the better.

As Erich helped Maud onto Beauty, his hand accidentally brushed against her thigh. Their eyes met for an intense moment.

"You want to ensure the reins aren't too tight; otherwise, she might pull away from you. If it's too loose, it'll be hard to control her," Erich said, breaking their intense moment.

"If she gets excited or goes into a trot, gently tug on the reins. To go faster, lightly pat her side with your foot and loosen the reins a bit," Erich continued.

Erich did a final check to make sure everything was in place.

"We're good to go," he said.

Erich noted that Maud quickly bonded with Beauty and suggested they take a quick trot nearby as a downpour seemed imminent.

They set off down the road and headed toward a nearby lake where Patrick had taken Erich fishing a few times. At first, Maud felt apprehensive about being so high off the ground, but she soon relaxed with the gentle sway of the horse beneath her and Erich close by her side.

At the lake's entrance, they quietly made their way down a long, wide avenue lined with tall chestnut trees. The branches above intertwined, forming a natural canopy that blocked any daylight trying to break through. The sound of leaves rustling in the wind created an atmosphere of haunting beauty. Erich sensed that Beast was nervous.

"Good boy, Beast, we're almost there," Erich murmured, gently stroking the horse's head.

As they reached the end of the avenue, it revealed a picturesque view of the lake. The lake sparkled under the burst of sunlight reflecting off its surface. The air felt warmer and more welcoming, dispelling the cold and dampness of the heavily canopied avenue they had just left behind. Erich and Maud had the whole place except for a boat with two men fishing in the middle of the lake.

An old, dilapidated two-story house stood by the lake, overlooking the water. Erich imagined what it must have been like during its heyday, waking up to such splendid views. Patrick told him that Michael Byrne had once lived there with his wife and four children but had immigrated to America in the early 1920s for a better life. The house and 20 acres of land that had been in the family for several generations, along with some livestock, were auctioned off. According to Patrick, the land was being put to good use, and the old barn behind the house was used to store hay for the winter. Yet, the house had been neglected for some time and had fallen into disrepair. The first time Patrick took Erich there, he fell in love with the place and felt it was somewhere he could live - a nice, secluded spot away from the outside world. Erich envied Michael Byrne for having the freedom to move so far away, even though it couldn't have been easy, knowing this might be the last time he would ever see his loved ones.

The past five months in Ireland had given Erich time to reflect on his life, particularly his life back in Berlin and the uncertainty of his future. Two months earlier, Mr. Fischer from the German Embassy in Dublin contacted Erich and informed him that their German U-boat had successfully landed off the coast of Galway, but the mission had failed. Two men from the U-boat ended up at a local pub and drank more than they should have. Coincidentally, there was an off-duty policeman present who got suspicious. The policeman observed that the more they drank, the more pronounced their German accents became, which led him to suspect they could be potential spies, so he arrested them. One of the men was Erich's contact, but since the plan hadn't gone according to plan, he was instructed to carry on as usual until further notice. Mr. Fischer cautioned Erich that a recent nationwide alert had warned the local people about potential German Spies in Ireland.

Upon hearing this news, Erich felt relieved that the mission had failed, but he felt guilty for keeping a secret from those closest to him. Over the past few months, he has grown very close to his grand-mother and grand-uncle and now meeting Maud has given him a fresh perspective! Erich wished he could cut ties with the Third Reich and begin anew in Ireland.

"I've been here before; it was just before my father died," Maud exclaimed, shaking Erich out of his reverie.

Erich helped Maud dismount from her horse and secure the horses by the tree. They stood at the edge of the lake, taking in its beauty. They observed some fish breaking the surface and coming up for some air. A large fish leaps out of the water, performs a somersault in the air, and then plunges back into the depths of the lake, creating a ripple effect. Then, a crane with its wings outstretched and its long legs dangling elegantly glided across the lake, landing briefly before taking off with a fish in its beak. On the opposite side of the lake, white swans glided gracefully along the lake's edge.

"Mother nature at her finest," Maud exclaimed.

Erich and Maud strolled along the lake until they reached a sandy spot. Erich removed his jacket, laid it on the sand, and gestured for Maud to sit down. They sat there silently for a moment, enjoying each other's company and the warmth of the sun on their faces. They played a game of throwing stones into the lake to see who could throw the farthest. This was a place that Erich loved to visit, a spot where one could lose oneself in deep thought, a hidden gem.

Barely an hour had passed when it started to rain, prompting Erich and Maud to leap to their feet, knowing they were in for a downpour. The nearest place for them to take shelter was the barn.

"Irish weather, when it rains, it pours," Maud exclaimed.

Erich picked up his jacket, handed it to Maud, and beckoned for her to go on while he took care of the horses. By the time he caught up with her, it was pouring rain. He managed to get the horses into the barn and tied them to a wooden support beam. The horses were nervous, especially with the deafening sound of heavy rain pounding against the corrugated roof. Erich eased their nerves by giving them some hay to nibble on. He reckoned they would be here for some time.

Erich's clothes were soaked, and he suddenly felt chilled to the bone, especially while standing in a cold, drafty barn that had clearly seen better days. Maud stepped forward, took his jacket from her shoulders, and handed it back to him.

"I think you'll need this more than me," she said.

Their hands touched, and their eyes locked onto one another. Despite the chilly draft around them, Maud suddenly felt warm and was aware that her face was burning. Erich couldn't resist but take her in his arms and kiss her tenderly. Maud wrapped her arms around his neck and held him closely, sharing a passionate kiss.

"It's drafty in here; we'll catch our death!" Maud exclaimed, breaking away briefly.

Without saying a word, Erich took her hand and led her up the ladder to the loft. He spread his jacket on the floor by the wall and gently pulled her down to join him. They leaned against the wall, holding hands, and listened to the heavy downpour, knowing it wouldn't let up anytime soon. Erich wrapped his arms around her, kissed her, and paused briefly to take her in.

"You are beautiful," Erich said softly.

Maud told Erich that she was still a virgin. He found her even more alluring and assured her that he wanted it to be special for her when the time was right. They sat there for what felt like an eternity, his arms wrapped around her and his chin resting on her head. With the sound of rain lashing against the corrugated iron roof and the warmth of her body flowing through him, Erich soon dozed off to sleep.

CHAPTER 24

Colin - Reflection

Colin's heart was shattered. Four months had passed, and he still couldn't believe that Maud had ended their relationship. He immersed himself in his work and kept a low profile to avoid her, given that he was living in a small community where the likelihood of encountering her was high. To avoid any encounters with Maud, Colin attended late mass on Sundays and stopped going to the local pub on Fridays. He couldn't stop thinking about what she had said to him the night they broke up.

"No, Colin, nothing happened between Erich and me. To be honest, I wanted it to happen," Maud said rather coldly.

It felt like a slap in the face, and to add insult to injury, he had heard through the grapevine that Maud and Erich had recently become an official couple. The mere thought of seeing them together would be unbearable.

Colin's parents became worried when they noticed how much their son had withdrawn into himself. They noticed that his social life had come to a standstill, and even more concerning was his lack of interest in his work.

"Son, it's been four months now. Don't you think it's time to move on? This isn't healthy for you nor is it for any of us. No one can say a word without you snapping their head off," his father exclaimed.

"Colin, you've got a whole lifetime ahead of you - only time will heal; trust me, it's not the end of the world," his father continued.

"Mark my words, son, one day you'll meet someone new, and Maud will be just a distant memory," his mother added.

Colin knew his parents were right; he needed to move on, and the only way to do that was to move as far away as possible from this place. He realized that the only thing keeping him here was Maud, and now that they were no longer together, he had no reason to stay. Besides, he had grown tired of farm life, and as the youngest son, he was not next in line to inherit it. He also found that living in a close-knit community where everyone knew each other's business was suffocating. Colin decided it was time to leave, so he enlisted in the Irish Armed Forces in September 1938.

At first, Colin's parents were dismayed to learn that he had joined the Irish Armed Forces but soon came around to the idea. His mother had a hard time letting go of her youngest son, who, in her eyes, was her baby.

"We are going to miss you, my love," she said, her voice full of emotion.

"Mom, it's not like I'm going thousands of miles away; I'm only moving to County Kildare. I'll be home often to see you; sure, you can come to visit me," Colin said, hugging his mother.

"Don't forget where you come from, and make sure you write to us," Colin's father said, placing his hand on his son's shoulder.

In the coming weeks, Colin said goodbye to his friends, with Maud being the last person he needed to see. This was the only way for him to let her go, closing a chapter in his life and moving forward. He called on her one morning shortly after breakfast. At first, it was awkward as they exchanged pleasantries. Maud was glad that he made the effort and wished him the best of luck for the future. The next morning, Colin left to begin training at the army barracks. To him, it felt like he was moving a thousand miles away, creating a significant distance between himself and Maud.

CHAPTER 25

The Wedding – April 1939

As the church bells rang, Maud and Erich stood at the church door posing for the photographer as he took photos of the happy couple. The weather was perfect – a beautiful sunny day. Family and friends congratulated the couple, and some bystanders paused to offer their congratulations.

Erich was grinning from ear to ear; he felt like the luckiest man alive, being married to such a beautiful woman. The wedding was a small and intimate gathering of family and close friends. On Maud's side of the family were her mother, Sheila, and her three brothers, John, Brian, and Ian. To her delight, John and Brian surprised her by showing up the night before the wedding. Maud's closest friend, Eileen O'Sullivan, was her maid of honor. On Erich's side of the family were Margaret and Patrick, along with his grandparents from Germany, Friedrich and Alexandra Schmidt. He was glad they could attend.

Erich ensured he sent his grandparents the invitation well in advance, requesting their presence on April 1, 1939. He also included a personal note with the invitation, as well as a picture of Maud and him:

Jan 10ᵗʰ, 1939

"My dearest Grandpapa and Grandmama,

I have met the girl I want to spend the rest of my life with. It would give me great joy to see you at our wedding.

Your loving grandson,

Erich Friedrich Schmidt"

Seeing her walk down the aisle took Erich's breath away; he couldn't take his eyes off her. Since Maud's father had passed away, her older brother John took it upon himself to walk her down the aisle. She looked stunning, truly a blushing bride. Her wedding gown was made of ivory satin, complemented by a lace bridal overcoat with a high collar. Her hair was loosely swept back, with a few curls escaping beneath the floral wreath on her head. The wreath was freshly made with spring wildflowers, such as daisies and lilacs intertwined with green leaves, and in her hand was a matching bouquet. Erich stood there beaming as he watched Maud join him by his side.

The priest announced:

"Dearly beloved, we are gathered here in the sight of God and in the presence of family and friends to unite this man and this woman in Holy Matrimony, which is to be entered into reverently, joyfully, and in the love of God. Into this sacred estate, these two individuals now come to be joined."

"Who gives this bride to this Groom in marriage?" the priest asked.

"I do," John said.

John stepped back from the altar and joined his mother by her side.

Maud and Erich's eyes locked on each other; he smiled down at her, and she smiled back. This was an emotional day for Erich, as this was the biggest decision he had ever made: marrying the love of his life. There was the uncertainty of not knowing what the future held, but someday, he would be required to return to Berlin as a German officer of the Third Reich. But in this moment, it felt so right to be surrounded by loved ones witnessing their joyful union.

The priest continued:

> "Let us pray, O Almighty God. You have created us in the likeness of love, reflecting Your image. Bless these two who stand before You. Guide them with Your wisdom and shine Your light upon them, so that as they journey through life together, they may walk as bearers of Your Truth."

"Amen," the congregation responded.

Maud handed over her bouquet to Eileen, her maid of honor. The priest proceeded to bless the rings:

> "May the Lord bless these rings you exchange as symbols of your love, devotion, and eternal peace."

"Amen," the congregation responded.

"As you place this ring on your partner's finger, I now invite each of you to repeat the marriage vows," the priest continued.

"I, Erich, take you, Maud, to be my lawful wife, to have and to hold from this day forward, for better or for worse, for richer or for poorer, in sickness and in health, until death do us part. This ring I give you symbolizes my love. I pledge to share my loving heart, willing body, and eternal soul with you," Erich said, placing the ring on Maud's finger.

"I, Maud, take you, Erich, 'to be my lawful husband, to have and to hold from this day forward, for better or for worse, for richer or for poorer, in sickness and in health, until death do us part. This ring I give you symbolizes my love. I pledge to share my loving heart, willing body, and eternal soul with you," Maud said as she placed the ring on Erich's finger.

The priest held up the chalice of wine and handed it to Maud and Erich.

"And now, please drink to the love you've shared in the past."

They each took a sip.

"Drink to your love in the present."

They each took a sip.

"On this wedding day, let us drink to our love now and forevermore."

They each took a sip.

"I now pronounce you man and wife," the priest declared, gesturing for Erich and Maud to face the congregation.

Everybody stood up and clapped their hands.

The wedding celebration was held at Margaret and Patrick's house that evening.

"Family and friends, we've come together to celebrate this happy couple's unison; let's toast to their happiness," Patrick said.

Everyone raised their glasses, and Patrick continued by offering an Irish blessing.

"Friends and relatives so fond and dear

Tis our greatest pleasure to have you here

When many years this day has passed

Our fondest memories will always last

So, we drink a cup of Irish mead

And ask God's blessing in our hour of need."

"Slainte," Patrick said, raising his glass.

"Slainte," the guests replied, raising their glasses.

After dinner, the men cleared the floor to make room for dancing. Some brought musical instruments: a concertina, a mandolin, a few fiddles, and some flutes. The musicians took their positions and began to play. Maud and Erich were the first to step onto the floor, followed by Patrick, Sheila, and Erich's grandparents, Alexandra and Friedrich. Soon, the rest of the party joined in. A few hours later, Erich signaled to Maud that it was time to retire. He surprised her by sweeping her off her feet and into his arms, then headed towards the stairs. Everyone clapped and cheered for the newly married couple. Erich carried Maud up the stairs to their bedroom, and once they crossed the threshold, he shut the door behind them.

Erich and Maud stood for a moment, absorbing their bedroom. The room was spacious, featuring two large windows adorned with floor-length cream curtains. A wrought-iron bed stood in the center, dressed with beautiful white linen bedding, while a vase on the bedside table overflowed with freshly picked daffodils. Erich was immensely grateful to Margaret for transforming his bedroom into a honeymoon suite. It had been a long and exciting day but also exhausting. For the past couple of days, they had been busy hosting family and friends, and now, alone on their honeymoon night, Erich and Maud were ready to consummate their marriage.

Erich sensed Maud's shyness and reminded himself that she was still a virgin. He decided to take things slowly; after all, they had a lifetime ahead of them to get to know one another. Erich wrapped his arms around Maud, and she leaned back into him, savoring their shared moment. She then turned around, and they kissed tenderly. Erich slowly began to undress her. First, he removed her bridal over-coat and let it drop to the floor. Then he started to unzip the back of her dress, but it caught halfway.

"Let me," Maud giggled shyly as she finished unzipping her dress.

The dress landed with a whooshing sound as its weight settled on the floor. Maud stood in her satin slip, the strap slipping off her right shoulder, revealing a glimpse of her ample bosom. Erich reached down and gently lifted her slip over her head. Maud stood there, truly a blushing bride in her undergarments. As Erich began to undress, Maud helped him unbutton his shirt. She paused for a moment, gaz-ing at him tenderly with her hand resting on his chest. Erich could wait no longer; he kissed Maud tenderly, and with a sense of urgency, he took her hand and led her to the bed.

CHAPTER 26

Maud – Reflection

Maud couldn't be happier; she couldn't believe how much her life had changed since Erich, a tall, handsome stranger, walked into her life at a crossroads dance a year ago.

She never imagined that one day she would marry a German; life was full of surprises.

She always thought she would marry Colin, her childhood sweetheart, but that wasn't meant to be. When Colin left and enlisted in the Irish Army, she felt the weight lift off her shoulders. She thought back to that morning when Colin stopped by to say goodbye. She was surprised to see him standing at the doorway in uniform and how handsome he looked. Maud realized it must have been hard for him to do this, especially knowing she and Erich were an item. She couldn't be happier for him, moving on with his life.

Maud fondly remembered the day Erich proposed to her. It was Christmas Eve by the entrance to the Abbey; Erich surprised her by getting down on one knee and proposing.

"Maud, from the first day I met you, and throughout the last six months we've been dating, I want to spend the rest of my life with you. I love you. Will you do me the honor of marrying me," Erich said.

At first, Maud was speechless and couldn't believe what she was hearing. Erich had just proposed to her, and she noticed the puzzled look on his face as he waited for her response.

"Yes, yes, I will marry you!" Maud exclaimed.

"For a moment, I thought you were going to turn me down," Erich said, sighing in relief.

"I don't have a ring, but I want you to have my mother's ring, which is back in Berlin. Are you okay with that?' Erich continued.

"It doesn't matter, as long as we're together," Maud replied, embracing Erich.

Erich reminded Maud that as an officer of the Third Reich, it was just a matter of time before he could be ordered back to Berlin.

"I think it would be good for us to get married soon," Erich proposed.

"How about a spring wedding? The days will be longer, and the weather will be nicer. If you get called sooner, we can marry earlier," Maud suggested.

Erich and Maud announced their engagement on Christmas Day after dinner at Margaret and Patrick's house. Sheila became emotional and cried, overjoyed by the news that her daughter was getting married.

"If only your father were here," Sheila exclaimed.

"Oh, don't, Mum. You'll get me started," Maud said, reaching across the table to take her mother's hand.

Margaret could hardly believe what she was hearing. She got up from her seat and joined Maud and Erich at their side of the table.

"I couldn't be happier for you both; what a beautiful couple you will make!" Margaret exclaimed, hugging Erich and then Maud.

"Ah, sure, you'll make a fine couple; you couldn't have picked a finer woman," Patrick said, clapping Erich on the back.

Maud also reflected on their wedding day, when they were surrounded by family and close friends. She admired her beautiful engagement ring, a sapphire surrounded by diamonds on a platinum band that had once belonged to Erich's mother and was now hers. Erich's grandparents had brought it from Berlin. It was a perfect fit.

Her wedding outfit was stunning. Maud loved the simplicity of the dress, complemented by a lace bridal coat that flowed elegantly over it. The intricate lace details of the coat added a touch of timeless charm, striking a perfect balance between tradition and practicality, making it ideal for a spring wedding. It was the same one her mother had worn on her own wedding day, stored for many years in the trunk at the foot of her bed.

She fondly remembered when her mother took the wedding outfit out of the trunk; it had a musty smell and had turned from white to an off-white with yellowish tones.

"It's been locked away in this trunk for so long; all it needs is a good soak in some bleach, a wash, and fresh air - it will be as good as new," Sheila reassured her daughter.

Sheila shook out both the dress and the coat.

"Your grandmother and I made this by hand. Lord, it took us

forever. Try it on," she suggested.

"If you don't like it, I can make you one," Sheila added as an afterthought.

Maud tried on the wedding outfit, and it fit her perfectly. Seeing herself in the mirror took her breath away. With her mother by her side, Maud suddenly felt emotional; her eyes filled with tears. She imagined her mother, a younger version of herself, in that very same outfit, and now she was about to marry and commit the rest of her life to Erich.

They stood silently in front of the mirror, deep in thought.

"You know, it was most unfortunate that your dad passed away so young," Sheila said, shaking Maud out of her reverie.

As her mother spoke, her voice quivered, and she burst into tears.

"Oh, don't mind me, a silly old fool reminiscing about old times," Sheila exclaimed.

"It's okay, mum. I wished Dad was here, but if it's too painful for you, I can wear something else," Maud said, hugging her mother.

"No, love. I want you to have it. I wore it, and now it's your turn. After all, that is why I have kept it for so long," Sheila insisted.

"I love it. I would be honored to wear it," Maud said, tightly embracing her mother.

When deciding where the newly married couple would live, Margaret insisted that Maud and Erich live at the farmhouse. She wouldn't hear the end of it and reminded them that there was plenty of room at the inn. Maud and Erich agreed to move in temporarily until they found their own place.

CHAPTER 27

War Is Declared - 1939

On Sunday, September 3, 1939, it was announced over the radio that Britain had declared war on Germany due to Germany's invasion of Poland two days earlier. Patrick, Erich, Maud, and Ian were in Dublin to attend the All-Ireland Senior hurling final between Cork and Kilkenny. They awoke to a heavy downpour beating against their bedroom window that morning. With the noise of the torrential rain and the cold dampness of their room, Maud and Erich were in no hurry to leave the warmth and comfort of their bed. It was a morning for making love, only to be interrupted by Ian.

"Come on, you two love birds. This is the last call for breakfast," Ian shouted, pounding on their bedroom door.

At 11:15 am, British Prime Minister Neville Chamberlain's voice came over the radio, announcing that Britain had declared war on Germany. The dining room was packed with people, many of whom would be attending the All-Ireland Senior hurling final match that day. Upon hearing the announcement, a deathly silence fell over the room to the extent that you could hear a pin drop! Shortly after

Chamberlain's announcement, the voice of Irish Prime Minister Eamon De Valera came on to confirm Ireland's neutrality.

"With our history, with our experience of the last war, and with a part of our country still unjustly severed from us, we felt that no other decision and no other policy was possible," De Valera announced.

After the announcement ended, the room was once again filled with laughter and the chatter of people excited about the upcoming game.

Erich was stunned, struggling to comprehend that Great Britain had just declared war on Germany, his homeland. What would this mean for him, a German citizen and an officer of the Third Reich now viewed as an enemy? He knew it wouldn't be long before he received his orders to return to Germany. Maud sensed Erich's quietness.

"Are you okay, my love? You heard our Prime Minister: we're a neutral country, so you have nothing to worry about," Maud said, gently squeezing Erich's hand.

"Do I?" Erich responded, abruptly pulling his hand away from hers.

Erich saw the hurt look on Maud's face and noticed that Patrick and Ian were taken aback.

"Forgive me, my darling; this is a lot for me to process right now," Erich said, taking her hands in his.

"The last thing this country needs is another bloody war! Haven't they learned their lesson from the last one - a war that dragged on for four years? And for what? Both sides fighting a losing battle, with thousands of lives lost!" Patrick exclaimed.

"Hear, hear," the guests murmured in agreement.

"I lost my nephew Martin in that dreadful war of 1914. He was just 16 years old when he died in the Belgian trenches. His excuse was that he wanted an adventure, to get out there and see the real world. What an adventure that turned out to be!" Patrick continued.

He recalled that it was on the brink of World War I when Martin and his best friend John sneaked away in the middle of the night to travel to Belfast and enlist in the Leinster Regiment.

"You had to be eighteen to sign up, but the rascals lied about their ages when they were only sixteen. Martin's friend John failed the fitness test; his flat feet saved his life, but at the time, he was devastated," Patrick said, shaking his head.

Patrick paused for a moment as if contemplating what to say next.

"And now, with this war, there's no doubt that we Irish men will be expected to fight alongside the bloody English – what a joke! We've been fighting for our independence, and now they expect us to join their side in this bloody war!" Patrick remarked with a cynical tone.

"Hear, hear!" some guests exclaimed.

"Those damn English!" other guests replied.

It seemed like the rain would never stop, but just before the game at 3:15 pm, it let up, and a burst of sunshine broke through the clouds. The hurling teams, men in red and men in black and amber were led onto the field by their respective captains. The atmosphere was great; people laughed and shouted encouragement to their respective teams. Erich set his worries aside and focused on the game. Shortly after halftime, the game was interrupted by a clap of thunder, followed by lightning, and then a torrential downpour of rain. Erich, Maud, Patrick, and Ian had to dash for shelter, along with hundreds of other spectators rushing for cover.

Despite being drenched and covered in mud, the teams continued to compete against each other.

"Rain or shine, the show must go on - those poor bastards, I don't envy the lot of them," Patrick said with a chuckle.

Patrick was thrilled; his team, Kilkenny, won the championship with a score of 2-7 to 3-3.

CHAPTER 28

The Telegram

On September 5th, 1939, the postman delivered a telegram from Berlin addressed to Erich. Erich was outside tending to the horses when Margaret came out and handed it to him. He noticed it was sent from Berlin and placed the telegram in his pocket.

"Aren't you going to open it?" Margaret inquired.

"I'll finish here and be in shortly," Erich replied.

When Erich entered the kitchen, Maud and Margaret looked at him curiously. Margaret gestured for him to sit down and offered to make him a cup of tea.

"Have you opened it yet?" Margaret inquired.

"No," Erich replied, shaking his head.

Patrick came in shortly, sensing the tense atmosphere.

"Ah, Jesus, what's going on?" Patrick exclaimed.

With a shrug of her shoulders, Margaret explained that Erich had just received a telegram from Berlin but had not yet opened it. She made some tea, and they all waited anxiously for Erich to open it.

It was a tense moment for Erich; he felt his heart racing, each beat pounding against his chest as if it might explode. The telegram he received was an order from the headquarters of the Abwehr, Germany's military intelligence service, instructing him to return to Berlin immediately. Erich knew this day would come; war had been declared, and Great Britain and France now viewed Germany as an enemy. Thoughts raced through his mind; he had no choice but to return to Berlin. He believed it was his duty to stand by his country; otherwise, he would be seen as a traitor, a deserter, and a coward - offenses that carry the death penalty.

"Erich, whatever decision you make, we'll stand by you," Patrick said, placing his hand on his grandnephew's shoulder.

"Perhaps it would be better for us, darling, if I go ahead first and you join me later," Erich said, gently squeezing Maud's hand.

"No, I won't hear of it. You are my husband; wherever you go, I go - until death do us part," Maud replied, withdrawing her hand from Erich's.

He couldn't imagine being away from Maud and felt relieved knowing he wasn't returning alone.

Maud found the prospect of moving to Berlin exciting. For her, it was a fresh start in life; moving to a foreign country, learning a new language, and the uncertainty of what lay ahead were all exciting. Before the war was announced, they discussed buying the dilapidated house by the lake. It was an idyllic setting and a perfect place to settle down and start a family. The only thing that held them back was Erich's ties to Germany, knowing he would eventually have to return. The telegram authorizing his return to

Berlin meant they would finally have their own place.

Maud had longed for their own privacy. Living under the same roof as Margaret and Patrick made her feel claustrophobic. As a newlywed couple, she was conscious of the lack of privacy when it came to the confined space of their bedroom. She was aware that each time they made love, their bed would squeak, accompanied by their moans and pants in the ecstasy of their lovemaking. She was sure that Margaret and Patrick, whose bedrooms were just down the hallway, could hear them.

Maud loved Margaret and Patrick dearly, but she found Margaret's constant fussing over Erich to be irritating. She also noticed that Patrick was very fond of Erich, treating him like the son he never had. She had to remind herself that, after all, Erich was Margaret's grandson, the son of her late daughter, whom she had lost so tragically in a car accident. She couldn't imagine what it must have been like for Margaret to lose her only child.

Since Erich received the telegram from Berlin urging him to return immediately, they had very little time to say their goodbyes.

News in Ireland about what was happening abroad was mostly through word of mouth and from loved ones living abroad. Since the announcement of the war and Ireland's declaration of neutrality, news about what was occurring in the rest of the world was largely censored. For Erich, Great Britain's declaration of war on Germany changed everything.

The hardest part for Erich about leaving Ireland, a country where he had truly felt at home for nearly two years, was saying goodbye to his granduncle Patrick and his grandmother Margaret. Erich reflected on how much his life had changed, especially after meeting and falling in love with Maud, the love of his life, and now his wife!

Just before they left for Berlin, Maud received a letter from her brother, John, in London, informing her of the terrible treatment of Jews in Poland. He included a newspaper article with the headline "Germany has blood on its hands" that highlighted the mistreatment of the Jewish people by the Nazis. Maud felt relieved that Erich was sympathetic to their plight.

Erich warned her about the anti-Jewish sentiment in Germany, where laws segregated Jews from the non-Jewish population, stripping them of their rights and rendering them virtually invisible in German society. He also cautioned her about the anti-Semitism she could face on the streets of Berlin.

"Keep your opinions to yourself; you can't trust anyone these days, especially in this volatile climate we will be living in - not even your neighbors!" Erich cautioned.

Erich understood that going back to Berlin would lead to significant changes in their lives. He felt uncertain about the future there, especially now that Germany had been declared an enemy of Great Britain and France. He also worried that Maud might be seen as a potential spy, but he reminded himself that it was something to consider only if it occurred.

CHAPTER 29

Berlin

It was the end of September 1939 in the afternoon when Erich and Maud arrived in Berlin. The day was beautiful and sunny, with clear blue skies sharply contrasting with the cold, damp, and rainy Irish weather they had left behind. As they stepped onto the streets of Berlin, Maud was awestruck by the sights around her. Tall buildings lined the wide boulevards on both sides. What intrigued her most was that each building was adorned with a large red flag featuring a black cross on a white circular background, its arms bent at right angles and pointing clockwise.

"That's the swastika. It symbolizes good fortune or well-being and has been recognized since ancient times," Erich said, pointing at the symbol.

Maud noticed that the people on the streets seemed unaware of the enormous red flags, with the swastika symbol fluttering in the wind high above their heads.

The streets of Berlin buzzed with people going about their daily routines. Maud noticed some hurrying while others paused to greet one another. People lined up to board the tram, patiently waiting for others to exit. Some people sat on benches reading newspapers, while others basked in the warmth of the sun. On a nearby street corner, a vendor was selling bananas. A young mother walked by, pushing a stroller, while her little boy lagged behind, dragging his feet and crying to be picked up. Unfazed by this, the mother continued on, ignoring his pleas. Maud also noticed many soldiers on the streets, some alone and others in groups, marching down the main avenue. Erich informed her that these were members of the Wehrmacht, the unified armed forces of Nazi Germany.

Maud was captivated by the rhythmic sound of their stomping boots and the way they moved like wind-up mechanical dolls. She was astonished by the people's reaction to the soldiers as they marched past. The crowd stopped in their tracks and gave them their full attention.

"Heil Hitler," the crowd shouted.

Maud discovered for the first time that this was the Nazi salute. Everything felt foreign to her. She felt overwhelmed by her experiences on her first day in Berlin. The city buzzed with excitement, its tall buildings adorned with Nazi flags and streets teeming with people, presenting a stark contrast to the quiet little village she had just left behind in Ireland.

Erich and Maud moved into Erich's apartment, nestled in a nice, quiet neighborhood. It featured two floors with a private elevator. The spacious rooms had high ceilings, making them feel even larger. To Maud, it was a mansion. When they pulled back the curtains, a flood of sunlight filled the rooms, breathing life back into an apartment that had been locked up for almost two years. The added bonus was that the apartment overlooked a beautiful botanical garden. Now that Erich has returned, he is not alone; he has Maud.

The following morning, after breakfast, they set out for a stroll to the botanical garden. Dark clouds loomed overhead, and sporadic bursts of sunshine tried to break through, making it feel as if it could rain at any moment. At the entrance to the park, Maud observed a sign that read, "The yellow benches are designated for Jews.

Shortly after entering, they noticed an elderly lady sitting on a designated bench, reading her magazine. As they approached, the woman suddenly became aware of the young couple watching her. She quickly shielded her face with her magazine and averted her gaze to the ground. As they continued their way, Maud observed that most of the local benches in the park were labeled "For Aryans Only," with hardly any designated for Jews.

Erich noticed Maud's silence and guided her to a nearby bench, where they sat down.

"I don't feel right about this either, my darling. Hearing about it is one thing, but seeing it for yourself is another. This is the way of life in the Third Reich," Erich said.

For a moment, they sat silently.

"I understand if you want to return to Ireland," Erich added.

"It's shocking how one race can treat another as inferior. It's just like how the English treated the Irish under their rule! I feel for the Jews," Maud expressed.

What matters is that we're together, and no matter what happens, I'll always be here for you," she continued.

Erich wrapped his arms around Maud and kissed her tenderly. It started to rain, and it appeared that a downpour was imminent. They quickly got to their feet and headed back to their apartment.

They didn't have much time to settle in, as Erich had to report for duty the next morning. After being away for almost two years in Ireland, he didn't look forward to wearing a uniform again nor greeting his coworkers with a Nazi salute. It didn't take long for him to get back into the swing of things, although, at times, he longed for the peace and tranquility of the Irish countryside. Above all, he felt relieved that his assignment in Ireland as a sleeper cell never materialized. He also felt guilty for keeping such a secret from Maud, but he was bound by an oath to the Third Reich, which should not be taken lightly!

CHAPTER 30

Learning a New Language

Erich arranged private German lessons for Maud three times a week with a girl named Ingrid. Ingrid was a typical German girl with blonde hair, blue eyes, and a stocky build. She was also a few years younger than Maud. Within two months of arriving in Berlin, Maud quickly grasped the basics of the German language. Practicing German with Erich and through Ingrid's lessons boosted her confidence. Additionally, Ingrid was great company for Maud, helping her feel less isolated and lonely. Erich was eager for Maud to settle in and feel at home.

"Not having a good grasp of German can isolate you even more, my darling," Erich stressed.

Maud acknowledged that he was right. Now that she was living in Berlin, it was crucial for her to master the German language, which was also important for their relationship; after all, Erich was German.

As Maud grew more confident in her German, she motivated herself to venture out alone, fully aware that staying in the house all day wasn't healthy. She explored the streets of Berlin to become familiar with her surroundings. Initially, Maud preferred to go out in the morning when it was quieter, especially when people were at work. During these times, she noticed latecomers rushing to work and housewives and maids running errands. Once she found her bearings, she ventured farther out of the city using public transportation to explore local markets in the surrounding neighborhoods. Additionally, she enjoyed sitting at a local café, sipping coffee and people-watching. She believed this was one of the best ways to immerse herself in the German way of life, a culture that felt so foreign to her. This was her way of showing Erich that she was independent and didn't want to appear too needy. When Erich came home, Maud would share how her day had gone, whether it was exciting or not. Erich, on the other hand, couldn't talk about his work because it was highly confidential.

Erich was excited for Maud but advised her to steer clear of large gatherings, particularly of big groups of soldiers. He reminded her of their first day in Berlin when they saw soldiers marching by and people giving them the Nazi salute.

"If this makes you uncomfortable, just pretend you dropped something and bend down to pick it up. Or, if there are shops nearby, turn and pretend to be window shopping, but do it discreetly," Erich warned her.

"If they hassle you, just tell them you don't speak the language. Once they see you're a foreigner, they'll leave you alone," Erich added as an afterthought.

Since moving to Berlin, Maud had to learn to adjust to the changes in her relationship. Seeing Erich in his uniform, looking so dashing and important, was one thing, but the hardest part was that his job often kept him away from her, requiring him to spend most evenings at the office, working late into the night. She worried that since he wasn't around much, they might drift apart. Maud reminded herself that this was his career, which required a lot of time away from her, especially now that Germany was in the middle of a war. One thing was certain: she couldn't bear the thought of being apart from her husband.

"For better or worse, until death do us part!" she thought.

CHAPTER 31

The Party Invitation

A 50th birthday party invitation for Mr. and Mrs. Erich Schmidt arrived in the morning mail. It was sent by Hans Rudolf Hoffman's wife, Erich's superior officer.

"To Mr. and Mrs. Erich Schmidt,

Please join us in celebrating Hans Rudolf Hoffman's milestone 50th birthday!

Date: October 28, 1939

Cocktails: 7:00 p.m. Dinner: 8:00 p.m.

We look forward to celebrating this special occasion with you.

With best regards,

Herta Hoffman"

Maud was excited about the prospect of a party, a chance to meet new people, and an excuse to get all glammed up. Since arriving in Berlin, they had kept to themselves, and with Erich being so busy at work, their social life had been nonexistent. However, Erich didn't share the same enthusiasm.

"Darling, you might find it boring. We'll mostly be discussing work," Erich cautioned Maud.

Erich observed the disappointed look on Maud's face.

"But at least you'll meet the officer's significant other," he added as an afterthought.

Erich thought to himself that attending the party was the last thing he wanted to do, especially since it was hosted by a high-ranking officer he disliked and whose political views he didn't share. He was aware that if he didn't go, his loyalty to the Third Reich would be called into question.

Maud was excited about her first party and thankful to her mother for insisting on making a couple of evening dresses to take with her to Germany.

"Young lady, since you'll be moving in wealthy circles, you'll need to dress to impress!" Sheila advised her daughter.

Maud fondly recalls flipping through fashion magazines with her mother for inspiration on the latest trends in Paris. Shortly after, they went shopping in Dublin to buy the fabric. With her mother's assistance, they chose two rolls of cloth: black and emerald-green, Maud's favorite color.

"I love it! It's not too heavy - it's perfect!" Maud exclaimed, gliding her hands over the satin fabric.

"This will be easy to work with," Sheila exclaimed.

Maud draped the emerald-green cloth over her body and examined her reflection in the mirror.

"Oh, my love, the emerald-green brings out the color of your eyes and complements the lovely pink undertone of your skin," Sheila said, admiring her daughter's reflection in the mirror.

Maud noticed her mother getting misty-eyed, almost to the point of tears. She swiftly draped the cloth over her arm and turned to Sheila.

"Oh, Mum, don't, or you'll get me started!' Maud exclaimed.

As Maud embraced her mother tightly, tears welled up in her eyes. She took a deep breath, sighed, and attempted to hold them back. Just the thought of them both standing in the middle of a department store, crying their eyes out - heavens forbid! Maud could tell her mother was excited for her. She had told the shop girls in the drapery department that her daughter was moving to Berlin.

"Wow, how exciting, moving to Germany, even in times of war. How brave of you," the head drapery girl exclaimed.

Maud could feel her cheeks burning and was certain they were as red as a beet. At that moment, she began to question whether she was making the right decision. What was she getting into, and how long until she would see her family again? She had to remind herself that she was committed to Erich, her husband, and wherever he went, it didn't matter; it could be Timbuktu. When they got home, Maud's mother began making the dresses, transforming the fabric into two beautiful, classic evening gowns.

Thinking back to that day in the drapery shop with her mother and their intimate moment together made Maud's eyes well up with tears. She tried to stop the flow but couldn't, and before she realized it, she burst into tears. She missed her mother and her brother Ian, wishing they were only a train ride away. Now, living so far away, she felt homesick. She reassured herself that feeling this way was normal and that she needed to get it together because her life was now in Berlin with Erich. After all, she had chosen to come here, even though Erich had given her the option to stay in Ireland and join him after the war. She set aside her homesickness and thought about how costume jewelry and a beautiful fur stole would enhance her dresses. One thing was certain: the new life she was leading in Berlin sharply contrasted with her past in Ireland; it was clear that she was moving in affluent circles.

CHAPTER 32

A Day Out with Ingrid

In her next German lesson, Maud was excited to share the news about the upcoming birthday party with Ingrid by showing her the emerald-green dress she planned to wear.

"What do you think?" Maud asked Ingrid.

"All I need is some nice jewelry and maybe a fur stole or shawl to go with it," Maud continued.

"It's gorgeous! It truly brings out the color of your eyes," Ingrid responded.

"My mother made this," Maud said proudly.

At the mere mention of her mother, Maud felt a lump in her throat, and tears began to well up in her eyes.

"Oh, I'm sorry; please excuse me," Maud said apologetically.

"It must be hard for you to be so far from home. I can't even imagine what that's like," Ingrid said, gently resting her hand on Maud's shoulder.

"I know the perfect place to take you; trust me, you will love it. There's a local market not far from here, but it only operates on weekends - well, tomorrow is Saturday, so let's go," Ingrid suggested.

"Well, Erich is working as usual, and I don't have anything else planned," Maud replied.

"Yes, let's go! I could use some retail therapy myself; it's been a while since I treated myself to something nice. You'll find almost everything you want at this market: shoes, coats, handbags, jewelry, household goods - you name it, they've got it," Ingrid said excitedly.

The next morning, Maud and Ingrid headed to the marketplace. They saw a group of Wehrmacht soldiers setting up long tables and displaying household items and clothing racks. Maud was captivated by the racks of fur coats, evening gowns, and men's suits. Ingrid wasn't exaggerating - there were countless items, including boxes of shoes, handbags, coats, dresses, costume jewelry, and household goods. Maud was astonished by the sheer volume; she had never seen anything like it.

"Where does all this come from?" Maud asked Ingrid as they strolled through the marketplace.

"From the warehouses. If they can't sell it to the stores, the items end up here," Ingrid replied casually.

"And the Jews, when they moved out of their homes, left behind a lot of their stuff," Ingrid added as an afterthought.

"Do you mean the Jews who were forced out of their homes against their will?" Maud said in disbelief.

"Well, they had to leave - now we have more work! They dominated the job market, taking all the jobs and hiring only their own kind. The problem with these people is that they're greedy and only think about themselves," Ingrid said nonchalantly.

"Now that the economy has improved, there is more to go around for everyone," she added.

"Yeah, kicking people out of their jobs has certainly opened up the job market," Maud said to herself.

Maud couldn't believe what she was hearing from Ingrid. She was speechless and didn't know what to say next, so she thought it best to keep her opinion to herself. Although she considered Ingrid a close friend, she was mistaken.

"You can't trust anyone, no matter how nice they are to you!" Erich's voice echoed in her head.

Ingrid continued to rummage through the piles of clothing and costume jewelry without a care in the world.

"Look, this would look great on you, especially since you're so tall and slim," Ingrid exclaimed, holding a black Chanel dress and a pair of costume pearls.

"I'll pass!" Maud said, politely declining.

"Suit yourself, I'll take it!" Ingrid replied with a sheepish grin.

Maud excused herself and left empty-handed.

Later that evening, she shared her thoughts about Ingrid with Erich.

"Darling, Ingrid was part of the youth movement; they have been conditioned to think that way. She doesn't know any better," Erich confided.

"If you want, we can get you another tutor!" Erich offered.

Regardless of her political views, Maud decided to stick with Ingrid. After all, she wanted to hang out with someone, particularly someone in her age group.

CHAPTER 33

The Birthday Party

Maud was excited about the birthday party, seeing it as a chance to meet Erich's work colleagues and their partners - an opportunity for her to connect with new people. For Erich, attending the event felt more like an obligation, especially since Hans Rudolf Hoffman was his superior officer. However, he acknowledged that this was a chance for Maud to meet and connect with others, particularly since his job left them little time to socialize.

Seeing Maud standing before him, elegantly dressed in a flowing emerald-green evening dress, took Erich's breath away. She looked absolutely stunning. The satin fabric draped elegantly over Maud's figure, accentuating her curves. The emerald-green color complemented her complexion, making her deep blue eyes appear even more vibrant. The three-quarter-length sleeves enhanced the overall appearance of the dress, while the V-neckline drew attention to Maud's costume jewelry: a pearl choker – a cherished gift from Erich. At the center of the choker rested an emerald stone, complemented by matching earrings. Her thick, curly hair was styled into a sleek bob, with one side pinned back by a decorative clip while loose curls cascaded down the other side, creating a chic vibe. When it came to using makeup, Maud opted for a natural look, as the use of heavy cosmetics was discouraged by the Third Reich. Yet, the latest fashion trends continued to thrive in Berlin, with women following the latest trends from Paris.

Seeing his wife standing before him in all her elegance reminded him of why he had fallen in love with her in the first place, just as when they first met at the crossroads dance in the spring of 1938.

When Erich and Maud arrived at the party, a butler greeted them, took their coats, and announced their arrival to the hosts, Mr. and Mrs. Hoffman. The Hoffmans smiled warmly and welcomed each guest, making them feel at home. A maid approached the newly arrived guests and offered them a drink.

Now that they were at the party, Erich felt like the luckiest man in the room with his beautiful wife by his side. Even with the sounds of conversation and laughter buzzing around them, for Erich, it faded into the background as his focus remained solely on her.

Maud observed that the room was softly lit, with vases of fresh flowers arranged throughout, creating a warm and inviting atmosphere that set the stage for a 50th birthday party. She also noticed that as Mrs. Hoffman welcomed each guest, her gaze was both warm and attentive as she scanned the entrance for newcomers, ensuring that no one was overlooked.

"Oh, please call me Herta. It's so nice to meet you," Mrs. Hoffman said.

"Hans, it's a pleasure to meet you," Mr. Hoffman said, shaking Maud's hand.

"Make yourselves at home," Herta said, gesturing toward the other guests in the room.

Maud observed that Herta was wearing a long, midnight-blue satin gown. A strand of pearls hung gracefully around her neck, and her blonde hair was styled in a bun secured with a silver clip decorated with pearls. In her hand, she held a slender cigarette holder, a stylish accessory that enhanced her overall look with an air of sophistication. She looked quite glamorous. As for the guests, Maud observed that some wore formal attire while others opted for semi-formal.

This was a whole new world for Maud, a stark contrast to the social life she was used to in Ireland. With a wide variety of drinks available - fine wines, schnapps, and beer - she didn't know where to start, so Erich helped her choose.

By 7:30 pm, all the guests had arrived, filling the room with the laughter of friends, colleagues, and family as a pianist played a mix of classical tunes and popular German songs.

At precisely 8 pm, the chime of the butler's brass bell echoed through the room, inviting the guests to the dining area. The air quickly filled with the rich aroma of the main course: roasted beef, generously marinated in sauce and accompanied by potato dumplings. An assortment of cheeses and artisanal bread also adorned the table. A separate table was set aside for desserts, showcasing the centerpiece of the birthday celebration: a Black Forest gâteau.

After dinner, the men retreated to the sitting room for a private discussion behind closed doors.

"Just hang in there, my darling. Duty calls!" Erich said, giving Maud's hand a comforting squeeze.

Shortly after, the butler led the women to the library and left them alone.

Like the other rooms, the library was softly lit, with vases of fresh flowers placed throughout. Maud was captivated by the towering bookshelves that reached the ceiling, lined with aged leather-bound books whose musky scent lingered in the air. She was in awe, having never seen so many, and she wondered whether any books had ever left the shelves, let alone been read, or if they were merely part of the decor. The butler reappeared, carrying a silver tray laden with after-dinner drinks.

The women sat on two large sofas in front of the fireplace. Maud found them friendly; some were her age while others were older. Although she tried her best to communicate in German, she realized that most of them couldn't speak English. Despite their warm demeanor, Maud reminded herself that this was expected, especially since she wasn't fluent in their language and their conversation couldn't extend beyond a few pleasantries. She understood that adapting to this lifestyle would take time and that she would eventually become accustomed to it.

As the night wore on, the conversation gradually dwindled. Maud found herself drawn to the flickering flames and the crackling and hissing of the fire, its warm glow lulling her into a drowsy state. She felt relieved when the men joined them, and slowly, the guests began to leave.

CHAPTER 34

December 1939

Nearly four months into the war, the German people were optimistic, believing it would be swift and lead to their victory - a victory their Führer, Hitler, had assured them. Through ongoing propaganda, the public was constantly reminded of their bitter defeat in World War I, feeling especially betrayed by the rest of Europe and Russia. The ongoing war is now viewed as retribution for the loss of their land, which was taken from their cherished German Empire, divided, and given to those who did not rightfully belong there. Moreover, the severe sanctions imposed on Germany by its victors led to high unemployment rates and rising poverty levels. Today, Hitler has created millions of jobs for the unemployed and has restored Germany's strength as a powerful nation once again. One was fully aware that the Nuremberg Laws, enacted in 1935, barred Jewish individuals from the job market and excluded them from German society, thereby freeing up more jobs for the non-Jewish population.

Since the beginning of December, Germany and Northern Europe have been plunged into arctic conditions, hindering the war efforts they had hoped would be swift and victorious. According to the latest news report, December was the coldest month Germany had experienced in over a hundred years. With an arctic front moving in from Siberia, temperatures plunged below freezing. The Little Ice Age, as it was called back then, reached its peak in the early 1800s, and now northern Europe has been plunged back into an "Epoch of Cold." No one knew how long this arctic weather would last, but concerns were growing for loved ones fighting on the front lines in such harsh conditions. Winter had arrived with heavy snowfall, effectively bringing the city of Berlin to a complete standstill.

Just before dawn, Maud stood by the bedroom window, peering through the curtains. She was captivated by the pristine white landscape that welcomed her from below and the steady fall of thick, fluffy snowflakes. There was that serene silence after a fresh snowfall, with no soul in sight or footprints. To Maud, it felt truly magical; it was breathtakingly beautiful, with the morning light struggling to break through the dark clouds. The entire area was blanketed in thick snow, covering the streets and lamp posts. One could barely make out the outlines of the road and pathways. The trees in the park across from their apartment were heavily laden with snow, with some branches appearing as if they could snap off at any moment.

Despite the frigid temperatures, Maud stood in thick socks with a blanket wrapped around her naked body. Erich was still fast asleep beneath a down comforter piled high with blankets. Soon, it would be time for him to wake up and get ready for work.

"Darling, we had heavy snowfall in the night. Oh, it's so beautiful out there - come and look," Maud said, gently shaking Erich awake.

"What time is it?" Erich groaned.

Eric noticed that Maud was excited, especially since this was her first experience with heavy snowfall. He struggled to get out of bed, and when his feet touched the wooden floorboards, a chill ran through him.

"God, it's freezing cold!" Erich exclaimed, trying to get his feet into his slippers.

Erich felt groggy, particularly after being abruptly woken up so early in the morning. He grabbed a blanket from their bed, wrapped it around himself, and shuffled over to Maud by the window. He opened his blanket, pulled her in beside him, and held her tightly. He savored the warmth of her body flowing into his and reminded himself that he was lucky to have Maud in his life.

They stood silently, watching the children below squeal in delight as they played in the snow. Two boys were having a snowball fight, a father and son were building a snowman, and a young girl lay on her back making snow angels. Erich hoped they would have children one day, but with the ongoing war, he felt it wasn't the right time to bring a child into the world.

It was still early; it would be another hour before people began their usual business.

"I don't need to get up for another hour," Erich said.

As Maud turned to kiss him, their blankets fell to the floor, leaving them exposed to the cold, frigid air.

"It's bloody freezing," Erich exclaimed.

"Oh, bloody hell, let's get back to bed before we catch our death of cold!" Maud exclaimed.

Erich quickly grabbed the blankets from the floor and hurried back to bed, joining Maud, who was now buried beneath the warm covers.

As the days and weeks passed, the frigid winter weather showed no signs of letting up. Maud saw it as a good excuse to hibernate; she couldn't bear the thought of going outside only to be met by the cold, harsh, blustery conditions. Due to the dangerous road conditions, people were advised to stay home unless necessary. Maud didn't envy Erich for having to go to work in such brutal conditions. With the ongoing war showing no end in sight, his job demanded much of his time away from home, often requiring him to work through the night.

CHAPTER 35

The Christmas Card

As Christmas approached, Maud found herself thinking more about her family. It was her first Christmas away from home, and the uncertainty of when she would see them again made her feel down. She was excited to receive a Christmas card in the mail from her mother:

"*1st December 1939*

Dearest Maud and Erich,

I hope this letter finds you both in good health and spirits. Everyone here is in great form. Margaret and Patrick send their love.

Maud, you are truly missed. The house feels empty without you, and it's during times like these that I wish you lived much closer. The boys will be home for Christmas, and I am looking forward to that. It's a pity you live so far away, and I know it's not easy for you to travel right now, especially given the current situation.

Stay safe, and love to you both.

Love, Sheila xxx"

After reading the card, Maud felt a lump in her throat, and tears began to well up in her eyes. She reminded herself to snap out of it. She wished she could spend Christmas with her family, but it wasn't easy, especially since she lived so far away and traveling in and out of Germany was heavily restricted. She truly missed her mother and Ian. At least Ian was there with her to keep her company. Maud often wondered how her brothers, John and Brian, were faring in England, especially now that Britain and France were at war with Germany.

Maud envisioned her mother and brothers celebrating Christmas together, gathered around the dinner table, enjoying a roasted turkey and all the trimmings. After dinner, they would sit around the fire, discussing the latest gossip and sharing ghost stories. She could hear their voices and laughter in her mind, wondering if they were worried about her, especially now that she was living in a country viewed as the enemy. She thought about her friend Eileen and wondered whether she was dating someone. She truly missed spending time with her and having their chats.

In the days leading up to Christmas, the harsh winter weather kept people indoors, leaving the streets of Berlin quiet and devoid of festive spirit. The only signs of the season were the large holiday posters featuring Santa Claus on a white horse, sporting a thick gray beard, wearing a slouch hat, and carrying a bag full of gifts.

"God Odin as a Solstice figure. Well, they do say that Santa Clause was a Christian reinvention of the Germanic God Odin," Erich said.

"This is the Third Reich's mission to discourage us from celebrating Christmas in the traditional Christian manner. Additionally, since Jesus Christ was a Jew, he is seen as no longer being part of our celebration," Erich continued.

"What banning the celebration of Jesus Christ, our lord savior! Jesus merciful God, what are they thinking?" Maud exclaimed.

Maud found this difficult to understand, especially since celebrating Christmas was a significant part of Irish culture.

Yes, we're encouraged to celebrate Christmas in a new pagan way - a Nordic celebration rooted in winter solstice rituals practiced by Germanic tribes before the arrival of Christianity," Erich continued.

"Winter solstice rituals, what does that mean?" Maud asked curiously.

"The winter solstice is celebrated between December 20th and 23rd, marking the beginning of winter and the new solar year," Erich said.

"We are also encouraged to adopt a new tradition: lighting candles on the Christmas tree to symbolize the return of light after the shortest day of the year and on top of the tree, a swastika to represent the sun," Erich added.

Erich noticed the uncertain expression on Maud's face, the look of not quite knowing what to make of everything. He embraced her, kissed the top of her head, gently lifted her chin, and pressed his forehead against hers.

"Don't worry, I'm not going all pagan on you. My grandparents and I still believe in celebrating Christmas the traditional way," Erich said reassuringly.

"Good, you had me worried there," Maud replied.

CHAPTER 36

Christmas Eve

It was Christmas Eve, and Erich and Maud planned to celebrate it with his grandparents, Friedrich and Alexandra. Erich sensed Maud's sadness while observing her reflection in the vanity mirror. She sat there in her slip, staring straight ahead, lost in thought.

"Darling, I'm missing a cufflink," Erich said, standing behind her.

Maud didn't respond; she looked as though her mind was a thousand miles away.

"Are you okay, my darling?" Erich asked.

Erich knelt beside Maud and noticed tears welling up in her eyes. He pulled her into his embrace.

"Oh, don't mind me, my love. I'm just feeling a bit homesick. I'll be alright. It's just one of those things," Maud said, breaking down in tears.

"Oh, Maud darling, I know this must be hard for you, especially being so far from home," Erich said.

Erich stood up, gently took her hand, and led her to the bed. He gestured for her to lie down, then lay down beside her, wrapping his arms around her.

"Darling, I'm sorry for not being around as much, especially with this damn war and my work taking so much time away from you.

"Do you want to go home?" he asked softly.

"No, you're my husband. I will always be here for you, no matter what," Maud said, gently stroking Erich's face.

Erich and Maud embraced, kissed tenderly, and made love. They fell asleep for a while, only to wake up and realize they were late for dinner.

"Crap, we're running late!" Erich exclaimed, jumping out of bed.

He called his grandparents to apologize for being late and to assure them he was on his way.

When Erich and Maud arrived, they were greeted at the door by an elderly butler. Earlier, Erich had told Maud that the butler, Otto, had served his grandparents long before he was born!

"Hello, Otto! How have you been?" Erich asked as he embraced Otto.

"We've missed you! It's been too long!" Otto exclaimed, excited to see Erich, and embraced him like a son.

"This is my lovely wife, Maud. You can blame her for keeping me away for so long," Erich said.

"It's a pleasure to meet you, ma'am; I've heard so much about you!' Otto said, shaking Maud's hand.

Although Otto spoke German to Maud, she understood very little of what he said.

"It's a pleasure to meet you," Maud replied in German.

Otto took their coats and went to inform Friedrich and Alexandra that their guests had finally arrived.

Standing in the hallway, Maud was captivated by the grand staircase. Adding to its splendor, a crystal chandelier hung high above their heads, illuminating the corridor. Maud was mesmerized by its beauty, especially how the light bounced off the crystals, making them sparkle and glitter. She had never seen anything like it before. She imagined a lavish ball scene from its heyday, with guests dressed in their finest attire - men in tuxedos and women in flowing, bejeweled ball gowns - slowly descending the staircase, waiting to be formally announced and introduced to the hosts.

Friedrich and Alexandra Schmidt were wealthy, residing in a mansion on a picturesque, tree-lined street in an upscale suburban neighborhood of Berlin. Both came from old money: Friedrich's father, Andreas, a Berliner, amassed his fortune in the steel industry, while Alexandra's father built his wealth in the textile sector.

Friedrich and Alexandra soon arrived, excited to see their grandson.

"I thought you had forgotten us, son," Friedrich said, embracing his grandson.

"I hope dinner isn't ruined," Erich replied sheepishly, feeling guilty for being over an hour late.

"It's so lovely to see you, my dear. I can see you're taking great care of my grandson; I've never seen him look so happy," Alexandra said, kissing Maud on both cheeks.

Otto appeared again to let them know that dinner was ready.

"Come on, you must be hungry; I know I am. Let's go eat!" Friedrich exclaimed.

Maud was awestruck by the size of the dining table, which was long enough to seat an army. It was elegantly set for four, with fine China, silverware, and crystal glasses. She also noticed a beautiful crystal chandelier hanging above the table, though it was smaller and less elaborate than the one in the hallway.

As they settled into their seats, Maud noticed the numerous paintings adorning the walls. The one that captivated her the most was a self-portrait of a beautiful young woman hanging above the mantelpiece. It bore a striking resemblance to a younger Alexandra, who stood gazing into the distance, adding an air of mystery. She wore a pale pink gown complemented by a lovely set of long pearls draped around her neck. Her long blonde hair was styled elegantly and adorned with a stunning tiara, making her look quite regal. Friedrich observed Maud gazing at the painting.

"I commissioned that painting for Alexandra's 30th birthday. Whenever I look at it, it takes me back to that moment in time. It feels like it was only yesterday. I'm also reminded of how much time has passed since then," Friedrich said.

"You, young ones, should make the most of it! Life is too short, especially now that we're in the midst of a war," Friedrich advised Erich and Maud.

For dinner, Otto served roasted goose with dumplings and red cabbage. For drinks, he offered a glass of red mulled wine and water. Afterward, they moved to the sitting room and gathered around the fireplace. Otto served them tea and a rich fruit bread filled with nuts and spices. To the side, Maud noticed a large Christmas tree adorned with candles and ornaments, with gifts placed underneath.

Afterward, they gathered around the tree. Alexandra handed Maud a long, narrow box wrapped in red paper and tied with a green ribbon. When Maud unwrapped the gift and opened the box, she was stunned to find inside a pearl necklace - the very same one that adorned Alexandra's neck in the portrait that had drawn her attention earlier. Alexandra observed Maud's surprised expression and smiled.

"This belonged to my mother, and since I don't have a daughter, I would like you to have it," Alexandra said.

Maud felt at a loss for words and overwhelmed by this heartfelt gesture, particularly a beautiful gift of sentimental value that she knew must have been hard for Alexandra to part with. Erich, meanwhile, received a beige wool scarf and matching gloves as a gift - practical items for this time of year.

Maud reflected on how her family celebrated Christmas Eve. The living room would be decorated with mistletoe and holly, and there would be no gift-giving, as presents were exchanged on Christmas Day. She envisioned her mother and brothers celebrating as they traditionally did each year. They would attend midnight Mass and afterward enjoy a light supper of salted white fish and potatoes smothered in onion sauce. Then, they would light a candle and place it in the window to guide Joseph, Mary, and baby Jesus on their journey to safety. Afterward, they would gather around the fire, sipping mugs of tea, sharing jokes, and reminiscing about their cherished childhood memories. Reflecting on moments like these with her family brought Maud comfort, yet it also reminded her of how much she missed them. Erich noticed Maud's distant gaze and gently squeezed her hand, pulling her back to reality.

"Darling, I think it's time to call it a night," Erich said.

CHAPTER 37

Ireland - 1940

On June 22, 1940, France surrendered to Nazi Germany, and both nations signed the Armistice Agreement.

"June 27th, 1940

Dear Mom,

I hope all is well and this letter finds you in good health. How is Ian doing? Is he being the man of the house?

You must be aware of the news by now: France has surrendered to those bloody Krauts, the rate they are moving; before you know it, they will be over here, God forbid! What is alarming is that when the Nazis arrived in Paris, the city had already been abandoned by its government. To humiliate the French even further, they were forced to sign the Armistice agreement in the exact location where Germany surrendered in 1918 - revenge for losing the first war.

How did they come this far? I assume you aren't getting much news about the war since it's mostly censored there. Seeing images in the newspapers of the Nazis marching down the Champs-Élysées and the look of horror and despair on the faces of the French people says it all! It breaks one's heart to think of those unfortunate people, their anguish, and what's going through their minds. I shudder to think, as I report this, it could be us next, our world ruled by fascist pigs! As I write this, it makes the hairs stand up on the back of my neck.

You are not going to be happy with John and my decision. We have both decided to stand up against the Krauts and defend Europe. Please don't see us as traitors to our country by donning uniforms for King and Country; we're doing this because we believe it's right to stand up against this evil. Mom, please don't worry about us; we'll look out for each other.

Your loving son Brian xxx"

Sheila stood silently at the kitchen sink, trying to make sense of what she had just read. Ian walked into the kitchen, whistling cheerfully, and noticed his mother by the sink, gazing off into the distance, unaware of his presence. He saw the letter tightly clutched in her right hand.

"Ah Ma, what's wrong?" Ian asked gently.

Sensing her anguish, Ian tenderly placed his arm around Sheila's shoulders and motioned for her to sit at the kitchen table.

"I think you better read this, son," she said, handing the letter to Ian.

After he finished reading it, they sat in silence for a moment.

"How could they? Wasn't it bad enough that your brothers went to England for work? Now they've gone and put on British uniforms," Sheila said.

Sheila paused for a moment, contemplating what to say next.

"What will the neighbors think? They'll have a field day. Mark my words: as soon as they find out they'll be fighting for King and country, Lord Jesus, we'll be the talk of the town. I can see them now, gossiping behind our backs and calling us traitors!" Sheila exclaimed.

"Oh, the shame of it. I won't be able to look them in the eye; I'll be walking around with my head hung in shame," she continued.

"Ma, who cares about the bloody neighbors, those nosy, good-for-nothing, small-minded busybodies," Ian replied.

"How can I not worry? Sheila said, pointing to the letter on the table.

Sheila placed her hand over Ian's and gave it a firm squeeze.

"Ian, all I have is you. For all we know, we might never see the boys and Maud again," she said softly.

The thought of never seeing her children again made Sheila break down in tears. Ian wrapped his arms around his mother to comfort her.

"There's probably a good reason we haven't heard from Maud in a while, especially since she's living in Germany. After all, she is behind enemy lines," Ian said, trying to console his mother.

Ian had witnessed his mother's heartaches, first when his two older brothers, John and Brian, moved to England, and then when Maud left for Germany, a country now at war with much of Europe. He deeply missed his sister and worried about her safety, especially given the situation in Europe. The last time they heard from Maud was last October when she wrote to let them know she had arrived safely in Berlin. Now, almost nine months have gone by without a word. With recent reports of Germany invading France, this is troubling. All Ian could do was hope for Maud's safety!

"As long as she is with Erich, he will take good care of her," Ian reassured his mother.

Ian was envious of his sister, enjoying a fresh start to a new life in a foreign country. He wondered if Maud was aware of what was happening in the rest of the world. As for Ireland, being a neutral country meant staying out of the war. Everything was largely censored - a tiny country cut off from the rest of the world.

"It wasn't long ago that we were under British rule - you were just a baby, too young to remember!" Sheila said, shaking Ian from his reverie.

Sheila remembered that it was late October 1921, in the dead of night, when she was abruptly awakened by the sound of urgent pounding at the front door.

"Open the door! Open up now!" shouted a man with a British accent.

"You can't imagine how terrified I was, a young widow with no one to answer the door but me," Sheila said.

Sheila's eyes welled up with tears as she remembered that moment under British rule.

"Well, I leaped out of bed, grabbed my shawl, threw it over my nightgown, and rushed to the door as quickly as possible. Saints preserve us; I was terrified of not knowing who was on the other side and why they were banging on it so loudly late at night," Sheila continued.

"I remember Maud, terrified, standing at the top of the staircase, screaming like a banshee. I yelled at her to go back and take care of you because I could hear you crying at the top of your lungs. All I wanted to do was run back upstairs and hold you in my arms, but I felt powerless to do anything. I just stood at the door for a moment, frozen with fear. As soon as I opened the door, an arrogant British officer, accompanied by a couple of soldiers, stood there, demanding that I step outside," Sheila added.

"Terrified, I did what I was told and stepped outside," she continued.

"Do you know anything about this?" the officer asked, pointing toward the village entrance.

"I looked down the street and saw a pile of burning tires and large pieces of wood blocking the road. I said, 'No, I don't know anything about this,'" Sheila recounted.

"Then I suggest you bring the man of the house out here immediately and clear the road," the officer insisted.

"Can you believe the nerve? I certainly wasn't going to let that arrogant bastard get the better of me! So, I held my head high, looked him straight in the eye, and calmly replied, 'There are no men under this roof, only a widow with two young children.' I pointed out Maud, sitting at the top of the stairs with you crying in her arms. With that, the officer grunted and marched off with his soldiers, continuing down the street and banging on other people's doors. The nerve, not even an apology - I felt like dirt on his boots," Sheila said.

"As soon as I closed the door, I fell back against it. The shock of it all hit me hard - I found myself sliding down to the floor, shaking like a leaf and bursting into tears, unsure of what to do, let alone think. Then, I was embraced by the warmth of my two beautiful children. I don't know what I would have done without you,' Sheila said, squeezing Ian's hand.

"Where were John and Brian during all this?" Ian asked.

"Fortunately, the boys were staying with your uncle James," Sheila replied.

The mere mention of John and Brian made Sheila burst into tears.

"Ah, don't worry, Ma, the boys will be fine - before you know it, the war will be over, and we'll all be together again," Ian reassured her, squeezing his mother's hand.

Ian felt a pang of guilt and thought that now wasn't the right time to tell his mother. Would there ever be a good time? He had already made plans to leave for England with his best friend, Peter, in early September, but he found it hard to tell her. He believed this was a war worth fighting for. The thought thrilled him; it was exciting, an adventure into the unknown that would give him a sense of purpose in life. Ian knew all too well that there was no turning back once he left for England and was aware of what happened to those who had gone off to fight in World War I. They returned home without a hero's welcome and were labeled traitors to their country. He understood this was a risk he was willing to take.

CHAPTER 38

The Bombing Raids of Berlin - 1941

On November 7, 1941, Maud was suddenly awakened by the terrifying sounds of bombings in the distance. She felt the force of the blast against the bedroom wall, shaking the room to its core. Maud froze for a moment, unsure of what to do. Taking a moment to collect her thoughts, she realized it was real. Terrified, she lay there, listening to the bombs dropping one after another over Berlin, wondering what to do next.

Instinctively, she reached over to Erich's side of the bed only to find it empty. For a moment, she forgot he was at work, just like many other nights, working through the night. With a seemingly endless war, Erich's job had become more demanding, requiring him to spend long hours at the office, working late into the night and sometimes even through the morning. Maud didn't know what kind of work he did and had learned not to ask, as he was bound to secrecy. But tonight, of all nights, she wished he were here by her side, holding her and reassuring her that everything would be alright!

As she listened to the distant, ongoing bombings, Maud knew

she had no time to waste. She needed to think quickly and stay alert. She jumped out of bed, grabbed the flashlight from the nightstand, hurriedly put on her boots, and took her bathrobe from the back of the bedroom door. In the pitch darkness of night, Maud navigated the hallway with her flashlight, making her way to the front door. Terrified, she could feel her heart pounding against her chest as if it might explode at any moment. While fumbling with the keys to unlock the door, her hands shook uncontrollably, causing the keys to drop to the floor.

"For God's sake, take a deep breath, woman. This is out of your control," Maud exclaimed.

She hurriedly picked up the keys from the floor and unlocked the door. Maud entered the hallway and joined her equally terrified neighbors, who looked just as confused and frightened as she was.

An elderly man stepped forward and offered some assistance.

"Please stay calm. If you follow me now, we will slowly make our way down the stairwell and head for the shelter. This is our only option. If anyone needs assistance, please raise your hand," he said.

An elderly woman and a man in a wheelchair raised their hands.

"Then I will need some volunteers," the elderly man continued.

The reaction to volunteering was slow.

"We must move fast; the bombs won't wait for us," someone said urgently.

Some people mumbled in agreement.

A few elderly men stepped in to assist. Everyone slowly made their way down the stairwell, leading them to the shelter beneath their apartment building.

Erich hurried home as quickly as he could. Just before dawn, he found Maud in the shelter with the other residents. They all looked exhausted. It had been a long night, especially for the young mothers trying to comfort their crying babies and small children, who were tired, hungry, and oblivious to the chaos above them. The moment Erich spotted Maud, he rushed over and embraced her tightly.

"Darling, thank God you're safe," he said, holding her tightly and not wanting to let her go.

For a moment, Erich forgot where he was. When he came to his senses, he looked around the room. He reassured everyone that the enemy's bombs had caused minimal damage to their neighborhood, as the intended target was Tempelhof Airport and the Siemens industrial area. A sudden wave of guilt washed over Erich. He felt guilty for not being with Maud during such a crucial time, and despite the limited time they shared, Erich felt as though their marriage had become like ships passing in the night!

In the weeks that followed, a series of bombing raids continued to rain down on Berlin. This time, the city was better prepared for air raid warnings, giving residents sufficient time to reach their designated shelters. For Maud, most nights were spent sleeping in her clothes, lying awake, terrified by the thought of their building being hit. Still, she felt reassured knowing that every apartment building in the neighborhood had reinforced air raid shelters in their basements, all connected by tunnels. This meant that if their building were struck, they would have a chance to escape to the next one. Each air raid shelter was equipped with makeshift beds, communal kitchens, cabinets stocked with food, and a first aid room. If the buildings were destroyed, Erich designated an alternate meeting place for them, assuming that Maud had survived.

Maud noticed that most residents in her apartment building were women, children, and elderly men. Many had limited English, but she spoke enough German to communicate with them. She quickly developed a friendship with Greta, who was a bit older than she was.

"My husband is serving in Poland. God willing, the war will end soon, and he will be back home. I miss him so much," Greta confided to Maud.

Maud noticed tears welling up in Greta's eyes.

"I hope so, too," Maud replied, gently squeezing Greta's hand and giving her a reassuring smile.

One night at the shelter, the entire building shook violently to its core from the impact of a direct hit. Suddenly, everyone found themselves in complete darkness. Initially, a woman let out a scream, followed by the terrified cries of children.

"Hush, hush, my love; it's going to be alright," some women said soothingly to their children.

A deathly silence soon fell over the place. No one dared to breathe as they sat in total darkness, listening to the terrifying sounds of the ongoing bombing raids above them. Many thoughts raced through Maud's mind. She was terrified and wanted to scream, but she knew it would do little good for herself and those around her. It felt like a death sentence hanging over them, and all they could do was wait.

The frightened children began to cry again, some hysterical while others wept in the arms of their terrified mothers, who did their best to comfort them.

Some individuals began to pray aloud, their voices trembling uncontrollably.

"Hail Mary, full of grace," some uttered.

"Please let this be over soon – I'm too young to die," Maud whispered under her breath.

It seemed as though their building had been struck, and only when they received the all-clear did they gradually and carefully leave the shelter.

A bomb detonated in their neighborhood, just around the corner from their home, causing extensive damage to numerous buildings in its wake. The sight before them was one of carnage: bodies lay scattered along the road and sidewalks, tossed about like rag dolls, resting on heaps of rubble, broken, bloodied, and some torn apart. The initial reaction was one of shock.

"Those poor souls who didn't make it to the shelter on time," one woman exclaimed.

Maud felt herself going into shock as the ground beneath her gave way. Her fall was broken by a kind gentleman who quickly grabbed her arm and steadied her upright. He guided her to sit on the edge of the sidewalk and gently lowered her head toward her knees.

"There, there, you'll be just fine, my dear. We need to get the blood flowing back to your head, and you'll be as good as new," he said soothingly to Maud.

Maud needed a few minutes to process what she had just witnessed.

"Thank you," Maud said, glancing up at the stranger before her.

"It's my pleasure," he replied, offering his hand to help her up.

"Anton Fischer," he introduced himself.

"Maud Schmidt. Thank you. It's a pleasure to meet you, though not exactly under these circumstances," Maud said with a wry smile.

She paused briefly before gazing directly at the man.

"Thanks again," she said.

"What is a beautiful young woman like you doing here all by herself? Do I detect an accent?" Anton asked.

"I'm from Ireland, and my husband is German," Maud said.

Maud decided it was best not to share any further information with this stranger, even though he appeared to be a kind elderly gentleman. After all, it was Anton who had broken her fall and prevented her from possibly splitting her head open on the pavement - she shuddered at the mere thought of it.

Anton insisted on escorting Maud back to her apartment. She felt grateful, fearing that if he left her alone, she might have another fainting spell. She learned that Anton was a widower; his wife had passed away a year earlier. Moreover, they were practically neighbors, as Anton lived just one floor below her. When they arrived at her front door, Maud invited Anton in for tea, but he graciously declined.

"Oh, thank you, my dear. That's very kind of you, but I really need to search for my cat. She gets frightened by loud noises, and it may take me days to find her," Anton replied.

"You know, she's the only thing I have in this world," Anton added, his voice thick with emotion, almost to the point of tears, but he quickly cleared his throat.

"Well, I bid you farewell, beautiful young lady, and stay safe," he continued.

"We must keep our faith in Herr Hitler; he will protect us. Heil Hitler," he added as an afterthought.

After Anton left, Maud stood there for a moment, speechless. When she closed the door behind her, she leaned against it, slowly slid down to the floor, and burst into tears. She wished Erich was here and hoped for his safety; for all she knew, he could be lying somewhere in a pile of rubble. What if, in the worst-case scenario, Erich doesn't come home? Maud felt like she was living through her worst nightmare. More than anything, she wished they were back in Ireland. She longed for the peace and tranquility of home, not this place full of strangers in the midst of a war behind enemy lines.

A week went by without any bombings, and people quickly forgot that they were still at risk from the enemy. Like most neighbors, Maud felt relaxed but had to remind herself not to become too complacent and to stay alert!

CHAPTER 39

Saying goodbye to Loved Ones

Erich was worried about Maud's safety as well as his grandparents', especially given the seemingly unending bombing raids over Berlin by the British and Russians. Initially, people believed that Britain was solely responsible for the attacks, but they were surprised to discover that the Russians were also involved. Erich's department was the first to learn this information due to their role in intercepting enemy communications. They believed the Russian defense forces were already weakened, particularly after the German Luftwaffe felt confident that it had successfully destroyed the Russian airfield and that Germany had reached Moscow. This was Russia's response to Germany's assault on its territory. Upon hearing this news, Erich feared that the Russians might soon be at Germany's doorstep, and his gut instinct urged him to evacuate his family from the country.

Erich remembered the day when a bomb exploded right next to their apartment building. Fortunately, their building wasn't damaged, but the thought of coming home to a pile of rubble with Maud buried beneath it made him shudder. That day, after the explosion, he found it difficult to return home since most streets were closed to clear the wreckage and debris. Erich recalled his heart racing, fearing the worst. When he finally reached home, he felt relieved to see that Maud had returned safely. However, he noticed she wasn't acting like her usual self. When she recounted the chaos to Erich, she broke down in tears. This reinforced for Erich, now more than ever, that he needed to get Maud and his grandparents out of Germany.

That night, they made love as if it were their last, fully aware that everything could change suddenly in these unpredictable times. Afterward, they lay in each other's arms, with Erich holding Maud tightly as though he were afraid to let her go. He sensed this might truly be their last night together because the longer Maud stayed, the greater the chance that one of them could be killed. It felt like they were playing Russian roulette. Maud sensed that Erich was lost in thought.

"What is it, my love?" Maud asked.

"You shouldn't be here. I shouldn't have brought you over. What was I thinking? We need to get you out of here," Erich replied.

"I came here of my own free will. I can't imagine living in Ireland while you're here," Maud answered soothingly, gently touching his lips.

"I could never forgive myself if anything were to happen to you. I even dread the thought of coming home one day to find a pile of rubble with you underneath it!" Erich said.

"I know someone who might be able to help us; it might be a matter of cutting through some red tape. I'll look into it tomorrow,"

Erich added as an afterthought.

Maud knew Erich was right, especially given the current climate and the recent bombings. She feared not just for her own life but also for Erich and his grandparents. Since the bombings began, with Erich working long hours often through the night, Maud felt quite lonely. Berlin was a city she found hard to call home, particularly in the midst of a war where she struggled to make friends and felt very isolated. At times like this, she wished for nothing more than to return home to Ireland and be with her family again. It had been nearly two years since they last communicated. Although Maud had written to them several times, she received no replies. She assumed that since Germany was at war with Europe, mail wasn't getting through, and vice versa. She knew her mother must be worried sick about her.

"I'm really going to miss you, my love. I wish you could come with me and leave all this chaos behind," Maud said, nestling her head against Erich's chest.

"I wish that too, darling, but if I were to leave, I would be viewed as a traitor. Do you know what they do to traitors? Just be patient; I'll join you once this madness is over," Erich said more seriously.

"I promise you," Erich whispered, gazing at Maud tenderly.

The next morning, Erich started organizing Maud's paperwork. He assumed that, since she was a foreign national from a neutral country, they would encounter no problems in obtaining permission for her to leave Germany. Erich wasn't particularly concerned about his grandparents, as their wealth would ensure a safe escape from Germany.

When Erich first spoke to his grandparents about leaving, they resisted, especially Alexandra, who was more reluctant to go than Friedrich.

"I'm not sure I want to leave at this stage in our lives and abandon this," Alexandra said, gesturing to her home and belongings.

"It's for your own good. I'll never forgive myself if anything happens to you," Erich said.

"Look, I lost both my parents when I was very young - I don't want to lose you too!" Erich added, this time with urgency in his voice.

Tears welled in Erich's eyes as he spoke, prompting Alexandra and Friedrich to begin crying.

"Well, it's going to be sad to leave this place. After all, I was born here, and three generations of my family have grown up here, " Friedrich said, glancing around the room.

"My darling Alexandra, we must leave. We can start fresh somewhere else, but unfortunately, we can only take the clothes on our backs and whatever we can carry," Friedrich said, holding both of her hands in his. Friedrich looked around the room and paused at the large painting of a young Alexandra above the mantelpiece. Tears began to roll down his cheeks.

"I'm sorry, but this is our only chance - it's now or never! I have my contact, but I need your papers and some money to get them to my contact tonight," Erich said, placing his hand on his grandfather's shoulder.

"I know, son, this is for the best," Friedrich nodded in agreement.

With the right connections and a little bribery, it didn't take long for Erich to gain his grandparents' approval to leave Berlin. By January 10, 1942, Friedrich and Alexandra had packed small suitcases and departed from Berlin.

"You want to create the impression that you're only leaving for a few days; otherwise, you'll attract too much attention. Since many people would do anything to leave Berlin but can't afford to, they might call you out," Erich warned his grandparents.

Erich also advised Alexandra to discreetly hide her jewelry. On the day of their departure, she wore as much jewelry as she could, most of which was cleverly concealed beneath her clothing. The night before, she had given some jewelry to Maud as gifts and some for safekeeping. Maud also helped Alexandra sew diamonds and precious stones into the hems of her dresses, as these would serve as their currency, since their money would be worthless elsewhere. Furthermore, the crime rate had risen, and muggings were on the rise, which made Erich fear that his grandparents might become easy targets. Erich and Maud saw Friedrich and Alexandra off safely at the train station, ensuring they boarded the train heading to Switzerland.

A month later, Maud received permission to leave the country. This broke Erich's heart as he realized he might never see her again. One thing was clear: having Maud and his grandparents leave Germany was the right decision.

CHAPTER 40

Ian's Departure - January 1942

Just before dawn, Ian quietly slipped out of the house to avoid waking his mother. A wave of guilt washed over him for sneaking away without a proper goodbye, but he knew this was the only way to avoid a dramatic confrontation. He had planned this a year earlier, but it was now or never. Ian left a note on the kitchen table explaining his decision. He knew his mother would disapprove, but he hoped she would eventually understand that it was for the best.

Sheila began her morning slowly. She was reluctant to leave the cozy warmth of her bed to face the cold, damp air that awaited her. Since the start of winter, the weather has been unusually cold, with heavy frost damaging much of the vegetation and leaving behind a bleak and lifeless landscape. It has also rained more than usual during the days and nights. Sheila finds this time of year disheartening, especially the long, dark, and cold winter months. She attributes it to age; the older you get, the more down you feel during this season. She refers to it as her winter blues. She also reminds herself that spring is just around the corner, and the days will soon be longer.

Although Maud had been gone for more than two years, the house still felt empty without her. Sheila was grateful to have Ian, who, despite being an adult, was still her baby. By late morning, she made her way to the kitchen. Sheila brewed a pot of tea, poached two eggs, and toasted two slices of bread; she was starving. Suddenly, it dawned on her that she hadn't heard from Ian. Typically, he would shout "goodbye" before leaving for work at 9 am. She called his name from the bottom of the stairs but received no response. Sheila went to his bedroom and knocked on the door but still got no answer. Upon opening the door, she noticed that his bed was neatly made, which was unusual for Ian, who typically left it messy. Returning to the kitchen, she saw a note on the kitchen table and immediately recognized his handwriting. She pressed her hand against her chest, feeling her heart pound. Taking a deep breath, she hesitantly reached for the letter, fearing what Ian had written. Sheila sat down, her hands trembling as she poured herself a cup of tea and opened the letter.

"January 2nd, 1942

Dear Ma,

I love you dearly. I'm sorry for leaving you so suddenly without a proper goodbye. I know you wouldn't have wanted me to go, which would have made it even harder for me to leave. I have been planning this for the past year, and the timing never seemed right until recently. As you know, with few job prospects in Ireland, I've decided to move to England with my best friend, Peter. Don't worry, Ma, we plan to stay with John and Brian.

Another reason for going to England is to help defend Europe against

Nazi Germany! Yes, I know that being Irish, what was I thinking? We hate the English just as much as they hate us. But think about it, Ma: if the Nazis defeat the English - God forbid - we are next!

I know reading this letter will be difficult for you, but I need to do this for my well-being and self-esteem. If I stay here, I feel like I have nothing to look forward to, and I don't want to end up like most people my age, who have nothing better to do than hang out at the pub drinking - not good for one's morale, right?

Again, don't worry about me. I'll be with my good friend Peter and the boys. I know this will be hard for you to understand, but don't worry; I'll be okay.

Love

Your loving son Ian xxx"

Sheila sat in disbelief, stunned by her youngest son's unexpected departure; she had never seen it coming. She never expected Ian to sneak away like that, which she found hard to understand. Gazing out the kitchen window, Sheila lost herself in deep thought. The dreary weather left her feeling down, prompting her to dwell on a sense of abandonment. Sheila poured herself another cup of tea and headed back to bed.

CHAPTER 41

Maud – 1942

They stood silently at the kitchen sink, Maud scrubbing the pots and pans from their Sunday roast while her mother dried and put away the dishes and utensils. The day was chilly and wet, and it was now raining heavily.

"It doesn't seem like it's going to ease up anytime soon," Sheila remarked.

Maud's mind was a thousand miles away; her thoughts were solely on Erich. She felt lost and uncertain about his well-being, fearing for his safety. Now that America had entered the war, she hoped for a swift end to the conflict. Her mind drifted back to her last moment with Erich when he saw her off at the train station on February 12th, the day she left Berlin.

Maud vividly remembered the night Erich came home and handed her a pass granting her permission to leave the city, along with a first-class one-way train ticket. It was a bittersweet moment. At that time, she felt relieved to be leaving Berlin, but the uncertainty of when she would see Erich again weighed heavily on her mind.

"I'll be fine, my darling; it's for your safety. Hopefully, this damn war will end soon; it's really dragging on!" Erich said.

That night, they made love, knowing it might be a while before they would see each other again - especially considering the uncertain times ahead. Before she realized it, dawn had arrived, and it was time for her to leave.

Maud and Erich stood on the train platform, their precious final moments together interrupted by the sound of an employee's whistle.

"All aboard! All aboard!" the station dispatcher shouted as he hurried down the platform, blowing his whistle.

It was time for her to board the train. With only moments left, Erich and Maud quickly embraced each other.

"Goodbye, my darling. Before you know it, we'll be together again," Erich whispered.

A sudden wave of anxiety washed over Maud as she feared this might be the last time she ever saw Erich. Sensing her hesitation, Erich gently led her toward the carriage.

"All aboard, all aboard!" the station dispatcher shouted again as he sprinted down the platform, shutting the carriage doors one after another.

Maud quickly boarded the train, and as soon as the door closed behind her, she turned, leaned out of the carriage window, and reached for Erich's hand. He reached up, barely able to touch the tips of her fingers.

"I love you," Erich and Maud said together.

Maud observed the people around her bidding farewell to their loved ones on the platform below. She also noticed a group of young children in the carriage next to hers, waving to their distraught parents below. Maud estimated the children's ages to range from as young as four to no more than ten years old. She gasped when she saw a man below reach up and quickly pull his little girl from the train's door window, only to lose his balance and tumble backward. Fortunately, his fall was cushioned by bystanders who had witnessed the scene unfold before them. Maud watched in amazement as the hysterical girl safely landed in the outstretched arms of the kind strangers, who then handed her over to her distressed father.

"I can't let you go. I'm so sorry. I can't let you go," the father sobbed, holding his daughter tightly.

As Maud witnessed such a heart-wrenching moment, she felt a lump in her throat and tears welling up in her eyes. It broke her heart to see parents separated from their children, especially at such a young age. She couldn't imagine what it must be like for a parent in a situation like this, having little choice but to let their child go with the uncertainty of not knowing when, or if, they would ever see them again.

Maud's train of thought was abruptly interrupted when the train lurched forward, emitting a chuffing sound as smoke and steam billowed from its engines. Suddenly, a cloud of smoke and steam engulfed the platform, obscuring the view of loved ones as they said their farewells. For a moment, Maud lost sight of Erich. As the dense cloud cleared, the train slowly began to move and pick up speed. She kept her eyes on Erich as he sprinted down the platform, blowing kisses to her. In an instant, like the blink of an eye, he vanished from her sight.

For a moment, Maud stood frozen as the reality sank in: the uncertainty of whether she would ever see Erich again. The train conductor soon interrupted her reverie by signaling that it was time for her to take her seat. Maud walked to her assigned first-class compartment, where an elderly couple greeted her. They exchanged pleasantries, and she soon learned that they were also leaving Berlin for their safety. She felt fortunate that Erich had arranged her safe passage, but suddenly, she became overwhelmed, and tears began to trickle down her cheeks. She quickly dabbed her cheeks with her handkerchief and felt relieved that the elderly couple was asleep. With the gentle rocking motion of the train and the occasional lurch forward, Maud suddenly felt drowsy. She leaned back, closed her eyes, and drifted off to sleep.

Once Maud arrived in Ireland, she promptly sent a telegram to Erich to let him know she had arrived safely.

"February 18th, 1942

My dearest love, I have arrived safely in Ireland. I hope we will be together again soon.

Yours always, your loving wife, Maud xxx"

One month passed with no word from Erich, leaving Maud worried and fearing the worst. She reminded herself that communication during wartime was challenging, especially since Erich was behind

enemy lines. Finally, Erich's letter arrived in early March, confirming
that all was well.

"February 21st, 1942

My dearest darling, Maud,

*As I put pen to paper, I find that words cannot express how much I miss
you. I felt relief upon receiving your telegram, knowing that you had arrived
safely in Ireland. On the day of your departure, as I watched the train pull
away and take you out of my sight, my heart ached, wishing for nothing more
than to be on that train with you.*

*Ever since you left, my life feels empty without you, and not a day goes
by when my thoughts are solely of you. I yearn for us to be together again,
but the uncertainty of not knowing when makes this separation even more
unbearable.*

My grandparents are settling in well in Switzerland.

*Life here in Berlin goes on as usual. As you know, I am busy with work,
which keeps me from dwelling too much on what-ifs. Please send my regards
to your mother!*

Yours always,

Your loving husband,

Erich xxx"

Now that Maud was back in Ireland, she felt a mix of emotions:
worrying about Erich's safety was one thing, but feeling guilty for not
being there with him made her feel as if she had abandoned him.

CHAPTER 42

Many Changes

Since Maud returned to Ireland, she has realized that much has changed since her move to Berlin over two years ago. One month before her return, her youngest brother, Ian, moved to London to join his brothers, John and Brian. Since then, all three have enlisted in the British armed forces and are awaiting deployment. However, Maud has noted that her mother has become more confident and outgoing.

Maud was delighted to see her mother taking great care of her appearance, particularly her sense of style, which struck a balance between youthfulness and maturity. There was also a noticeable spring in her step now that she was dating Paul, whom she had recently met at a church-organized social gathering - finally, someone to share her life with, as it had long been overdue. Additionally, Maud's best friend, Eileen O'Sullivan, married a local man and is now Mrs. Byrne, happily raising their twin daughters, Aisling and Maire. With so many changes, Maud felt that life had significantly progressed for everyone.

Sheila couldn't be happier to have her daughter Maud back home, as she had felt quite lonely with the house to herself. Just as she had grown accustomed to Maud's absence, her youngest son, Ian, unexpectedly left. He departed in the early hours of the morning, leaving a note that explained he was heading to England in search of a better life. Sheila never saw this coming: her youngest son following in his older brother's footsteps. Who could blame him? The pain of his absence was unbearable; in her eyes, he would always be her baby. Feeling lonely in an empty house, Sheila made a conscious effort to go out more often. She became increasingly involved with the church and regularly attended social events. At a recent event, Paul asked her out, and they have been dating for nearly two months.

Now that Maud was back, it felt good to have some company again. It took Sheila a few days to share the news of her new love with Maud. She felt somewhat foolish, especially for a woman her age falling in love, but she was relieved that Maud was genuinely happy for her. Not long after Maud returned to Ireland, Sheila noticed her daughter's morning sickness and loss of appetite.

"I think you are with child, my love," Sheila told Maud.

Maud didn't know whether to laugh or cry. After missing her period for three months, she attributed it to the stress of being separated from Erich. Maud felt delighted about the prospect of becoming a mother, but at the same time, she was anxious that Erich was unaware. She put pen to paper.

"*March 20th, 1942*

My beloved Erich,

Last week, I received your letter, and my words cannot express how much I miss you. I have wonderful news to share: you are going to be a father! I'm about three months along in my pregnancy. Not a day goes by without my thoughts being solely of you. Now that our child is growing inside me, it comforts me to know that a part of you is deep within me.

It's good to hear that your grandparents have arrived safely in Switzerland. I wish them all the best.

Now that I'm back in Ireland, I feel that so much has changed since I moved to Berlin. For one, my mother has started dating someone she met at a church event. Can you believe it? I'm so delighted for her. Meanwhile, Ian has joined my brothers, John and Brian, in England, and all three have enlisted in the British Armed Forces, awaiting deployment. It broke my mother's heart. We hope and pray for their safety, as far too many lives are being lost in this war. As for Patrick and Margaret, they are doing well and send their love.

I sincerely hope this letter finds you, especially now that you are behind enemy lines. One can only wish and pray that this war ends soon and that we will be together again.

Your loving wife,

Maud xxx"

As the months passed, more information emerged from Europe: rumors of concentration camps, the horrific treatment of prisoners, and thousands of Jews being rounded up and sent to their deaths. Maud knew that Erich was not complicit in these hideous crimes against humanity; he was a good person, but unfortunately, he was on the wrong side. She also thought of her three brothers, Ian, John, and Brian, who had joined the British Army. She prayed for their safety, knowing it was only a matter of time before they would be deployed to Europe.

CHAPTER 43

The Gestapo Headquarters – October 1944

Shortly after midnight, Erich was awakened by a fist pounding on his cell door.

"Wake up, wake up," shouted the Gestapo agent, fumbling for his keys on the other side as he struggled to unlock the door.

The door swung open, and the Gestapo agent entered.

"Hurry up and get dressed; we're moving out tonight," he ordered.

The bright glare of the Gestapo agent's flashlight temporarily blinded Erich. He felt disoriented and dazed, especially after being awakened in the middle of the night. He could hear a lot of commotion in the hallway as the Gestapo agents moved from cell to cell, ordering the prisoners to get up. With the various sounds echoing off the prison walls in the dead of night, Erich felt as though he was living his worst nightmare.

Erich did his best to mentally block out the chaotic sounds - the barking dogs, the Gestapo agents shouting, and the moans and groans of confused prisoners - but it was impossible. He reminded himself to stay strong. He learned that Christian Fritz, a senior officer in his early sixties, had passed away in the middle of the night. After spending fifteen days in a cold, dark, damp cell, it had taken a toll on him. Fritz's first suicide attempt was unsuccessful; ultimately, it was his heart that failed. A week earlier, four prisoners had taken their own lives. For Erich and the others, their lives now hung in the balance due to the uncertainty of what lay ahead. The only thing that kept him going was the hope of being reunited one day with his wife, Maud.

The Gestapo agents quickly got the prisoners moving, as their only possessions were the worn-out clothing they wore day and night. Once the cells were emptied, the prisoners were instructed to line up in a single file. They were then guided by the beams of the Gestapo agents' flashlights, with one agent at the front and another at the back. Erich felt overwhelmed; even the mere thought of not knowing what lay ahead filled him with dread.

Erich and fifty other prisoners soon found themselves in the vast open courtyard. He saw trucks lined up at the side, prepared to be loaded with prisoners. They stood in line, shivering in the frigid cold of the night, surrounded by a dozen or more Gestapo agents and their barking dogs. As they waited, it felt like they were trapped in a wind tunnel, with gusts of wind sending chills deep into their bones. It was unbearable.

The prisoners were forcibly pushed onto the trucks.

"Schnell, schnell" the Gestapo agent shouted.

Those who couldn't move fast enough felt the butt of the Gestapo agent's rifle!

"Where are we going? I have the right to know," one of the prisoners shouted in frustration.

Instead of getting a response, the prisoner was struck on the side of his head with the butt of a rifle, causing him to lose his balance. Erich and another prisoner quickly helped break his fall by leaning in, allowing him to take their weight. They acted out of fear that he might be sidelined and shot.

The trucks were now loaded with prisoners crammed into dark, confined spaces. A Gestapo agent warned them not to communicate with one another and that any attempts to escape would result in death.

The trucks left in convoys, creating a considerable distance between the prisoners and the Gestapo headquarters. Two Gestapo agents on motorbikes were assigned to each truck to ensure that no prisoners could escape. Erich overheard one Gestapo agent telling the other that it was 2 am and they were in for a long day.

The prisoners, too exhausted, sat motionless with their heads bowed and arms folded, trying to stay warm. Despite the air being thick with the stench of unwashed bodies and dirty clothes, many prisoners managed to fall asleep, lulled by the gentle sway of the truck, even as they hit the occasional pothole and experienced jolts. For some, the smell of fear lingered in the air - the dread of not knowing what fate awaited them.

After what felt like an eternity on the road, the first light of dawn began to filter through the gaps in the truck's thick canopy curtains. Through these openings, Erich caught sight of a road sign indicating they were heading toward Bavaria. He quickly realized they were on their way to the Flossenbürg concentration camp, located near the Czechoslovakian border. Erich knew the camp was initially set up for male prisoners to quarry granite in the nearby hills. Now, it operates as a manufacturing facility that produces aircraft parts for fighter planes.

Only after they reached the countryside did the trucks come to a complete stop. Both the prisoners and the Gestapo agents welcomed the break, an opportunity to stretch their legs and relieve themselves. The Gestapo agents closely monitored the prisoners as they tended to their needs while also keeping a watchful eye on the road. The vast, open fields of farmland and a few distant houses provided no hiding places for the prisoners, rendering any attempts to escape futile.

At one point, a man and a woman in a horse-drawn cart piled high with wood slowly passed by, their curiosity getting the better of them as they observed the prisoners surrounded by Gestapo agents. When a Gestapo agent menacingly approached them, they felt threatened and moved on. At that moment, two prisoners decided to make a run for it but were shot in the back. The other prisoners held their breath as they watched their fellow prisoners plunge headfirst into the ditch filled with muddy water. Then, they observed in horror as they struggled to breathe until they finally succumbed to death.

"That'll teach them a lesson," the Gestapo agent remarked after he shot them in the back.

CHAPTER 44

Flossenbürg Concentration Camp –
October 1944

In the early afternoon, a convoy of trucks arrived at the Flossenbürg concentration camp. Despite the cramped conditions, Erich managed to get some rest. He could hear the SS guards greeting the Gestapo agents at the gate.

"Heil Hitler," they said, clicking their boots in unison.

After a brief exchange of greetings, the grinding sound of heavy metal gates opening soon followed. Once the gates opened, the trucks lurched forward for a moment before coming to a complete stop. The heavy gates slammed shut behind them with a resounding clang that echoed through the air, severing their connection to the outside world. A chill ran down Erich's spine, causing the hairs on the back of his neck to stand up.

The heavy covers of the truck were pulled back, and a sudden burst of afternoon sunlight flooded in, momentarily blinding Erich and the other prisoners. A Gestapo agent stood below, shouting orders for the prisoners to disembark. Those who were too dazed or slow to move met the receiving end of his baton. Before long, all the trucks were surrounded by the SS guards from the camp.

"Schnell, schnell," they shouted.

Some were all too eager to strike at the prisoners with their batons or the butts of their rifles, swinging wildly as the prisoners hurried off the trucks.

Once the trucks were unloaded, the Gestapo agents departed for Berlin. Erich noticed the camp's commanding officer standing on the sidelines, observing the chaotic scene unfolding before him. The courtyard was now filled with terrified prisoners trying to shield themselves from the blows of the SS guards and their menacing guard dogs, which their handlers struggled to control. The snarling dogs lunged forward, baring their teeth and poised to attack on command. Erich shuddered at the thought of the serious harm they could inflict on a prisoner if unleashed. Once the commotion subsided, the prisoners stood obediently in line, waiting for inspection.

The commanding officer paced back and forth; his cold gray eyes reflected nothing but contempt for the prisoners. Holding a whip, he appeared ready to strike anyone at any moment.

"You all know why you're here. You're traitors, a disgrace to our Führer and our country. You're going to get what you deserve," he said.

"I guarantee you will never leave this place. Some of you will face a slow and agonizing death," he added.

A chilling silence enveloped the prisoners. They stood still, some staring at their shoes while others gazed into the distance. No one dared to make eye contact with the officer, knowing all too well they would end up on the receiving end of his whip. Without warning, the officer lashed out with his whip, striking Erich and another prisoner.

"I demand respect from all of you. Don't ever, ever look at me when I'm talking to you. Do you hear me?" he shouted.

The touch of the whip on Erich's skin stung intensely. He felt blood trickling down his face, seeping into his mouth and leaving a metallic taste. Instinctively, he felt the urge to spit it out but thought better of it. He didn't flinch, as he didn't want to show any signs of weakness. Instead, he stared ahead; his expression reflected resilience.

The officer stood face-to-face with Erich, waiting for his reaction. Without warning, the officer suddenly drew his gun and shot the prisoner next to him at close range.

"This is what happens when you disrespect your superiors," he remarked.

The officer returned his gun to its holster. With a click of his boots, he turned sharply to the SS guards and commanded them to proceed before walking away.

Erich didn't realize he had been holding his breath for so long until he finally exhaled; the mere thought that it could have been him on the receiving end of the bullet shocked him.

Under heavy guard, the prisoners were taken to a sub-camp of Flossenbürg, specifically designated for individuals involved in the resistance movement and accused of participating in the July 20 plot against Hitler. Erich soon learned that after the July 20 plot, many people were arrested and sent here, ultimately ending up on death row. With the prospect of a life sentence looming over him, Erich clung to the hope that the war would soon come to an end.

The next morning, the prisoners were forced to witness the hanging of five men who suffered a slow and agonizing death. They quickly learned from other prisoners that executions occurred regularly, either by hanging or firing squad. A few days later, two prisoners tried to commit suicide by running at the electric fence with full force, hoping to die instantly on impact. One person died instantly from the electric shock that coursed through his body, while the other survived but was shot right away.

Erich felt relieved to be assigned kitchen duties, where he helped distribute food to the prisoners. There, he met Father Rudolph Schafer, a German Catholic priest. Father Schafer's crime was his involvement in the German Resistance movement, which sought to overthrow the Third Reich. During his Sunday sermons, he openly criticized the government, telling his congregation that the Third Reich was led by a madman he described as the son of the devil, who should be put on trial for his crimes against humanity. Father Schafer was arrested in July 1943 and imprisoned in the same facility where Erich had recently been held and then transferred to Flossenbürg. Erich quickly bonded with Father Schafer, whom he saw as a father figure. Despite the limited conversations among the prisoners, he felt he could trust him. Erich also noticed that his prison block included several other distinguished inmates, such as German aristocrats, high-ranking officers, and clerks who served them.

Erich quickly adjusted to the camp's routine but mainly kept to himself. He frequently felt frustrated by being constantly under the watchful eyes of the guards. He felt humiliated for having to avoid eye contact with the guards or any superior officer, fearing he might receive a beating. The only thing that kept him going was his thoughts of Maud and his desire to be with her in Ireland. He had to survive for Maud's sake, as he had promised to see her again.

He clung to the hope that the rumors he had heard while working in the kitchen were true: Germany was losing the war, and its enemies were almost at its door.

CHAPTER 45

Sub-camp of Flossenbürg

To Erich, if there ever was a place called Hell, it was Flossenbürg concentration camp. Although a few months had passed since his arrival, it felt like an eternity, especially as he witnessed the brutality inflicted on the prisoners by the guards. Additionally, the prisoners were compelled to witness the executions at sunset, where ten wooden posts were erected on a raised platform in the center of the courtyard, making the grim events visible to the observers. Depending on the mood of the SS officer, prisoners were either hanged or tied to posts to face a firing squad. This acted as a stark reminder to Erich and his fellow prisoners that any one of them could be next.

The prisoners stood before the platform, encircled by SS guards and their barking dogs, as they awaited the execution of eight prisoners of war. Captured in France, the prisoners consisted of two British, one American, and five French resistance fighters. They walked in a single file, accompanied by eight SS guards and their executioners. One of the prisoners attempted to resist, only to be struck on the head and dragged the rest of the way on his feet, screaming.

Nearby, another group of SS guards started beating their drums, their rhythm nearly drowning out the unsettling sound of the barking dogs.

"You assholes, we're supposed to be protected under the Geneva Convention; you'll never get away with this, you mother fuckers!" the American prisoner cried out.

"Fuck you, Krauts, you'll get what's coming to you. May you all rot in hell," the English prisoner shouted as he was about to be tied to his post.

Another English prisoner spat in the face of the SS guard, who responded with a sharp slap across his face.

Erich empathized with those facing execution; despite their fate, he couldn't help but admire their defiant posture with their heads held high. Yet, he felt his anger rising within him as he, along with his fellow prisoners, stood helplessly watching an event beyond their control.

As the eight SS guards assumed their positions in front of the posts occupied by eight prisoners, who were now securely bound with rope and unable to move, the drums began to roll again.

"If there is a God, where is he when we need him?" one of the prisoners cried out, and then he began to sob uncontrollably.

"There is no God!" another yelled.

The SS guards aimed their guns at the prisoners.

"On the count of 1, 2, 3, 4, 5, 6, 7, 8, 9, 10, aim, fire," shouted the commanding SS officer.

The bullets tore through the prisoners, sending a spray of flesh and blood to splatter those standing nearby. Some prisoners died instantly, while others took longer to die. Some of the SS guards were overly eager to continue firing long after their victims had perished.

A deathly silence enveloped the courtyard. Erich felt the sting of tears streaming down his cheeks as he stood there, powerless, witnessing people's lives being taken from them in such a cruel manner. He reflected that prisoners of war were supposed to be protected by the Geneva Convention, and Germany would have much to answer for if they lost this war. The lifeless bodies were left on the posts to decay, serving as a grim reminder that no one knew what tomorrow might hold; it could be their last!

It wasn't just the executions that affected Erich; it was also the brutal beatings he witnessed daily, especially during roll calls at the end of the day. He was punished merely for making eye contact and forced to stand at attention for hours, from morning until evening sundown. Prisoners were frequently chosen at random and faced either a brutal beating or a bullet to the head. Those caught trying to escape were paraded in front of the others and executed, serving as a deterrent. Erich suspected this was just entertainment for the SS guards, as he had seen them standing around afterward, laughing and joking as if nothing unusual had occurred. Erich thought to himself that there could be no other explanation for such cruel behavior except madness!

Some prisoners had reached a breaking point, clearly visible in their eyes as if their souls had long departed, leaving only an empty shell. In their desperation, some hurled themselves against the electric fence, fully aware of the violent and painful death that awaited them. For Erich, witnessing the lethal voltage surge violently through his fellow prisoner's body felt like he was nearing a breaking point. The sight of SS guards reveling in the spectacle filled him with anger and disgust. Erich began to question his faith: if there is a God, where is He?

CHAPTER 46

The Planned Escape – December 1944

Within weeks of arriving at the Flossenbürg concentration camp, Erich formed a strong bond with Herman and Karl. By mid-November, they shared their escape plan with him.

Herman and Karl worked at the local arms factory, assembling components for fighter planes. Together with their fellow prisoners, they deliberately sabotaged the airplane components, rendering them unusable. This was their way of retaliating against their unjust circumstances.

Their crime was openly opposing Hitler's ideology. Herman, a former local newspaper editor, refused to publish what he deemed propaganda, and Karl, a teacher, was reported for being overly vocal in his disagreement with the Third Reich. Herman and Karl were both confident that their plan would succeed.

Herman and Karl familiarized themselves with their surroundings. The factory where they worked was adjacent to a forest stretching for miles, providing an ideal escape route where one could easily lose oneself and remain hidden for days. Fortunately, Hans, the supervisor on the factory floor, was on their side, giving them a better chance of escaping. The plan was for Hans to buy them some time by delaying the alarm about their absence. This delay tactic would occur shortly after their break, giving Herman and Karl a significant head start before Hans notifies the guards of their absence. With Hans's assurance, they believed this was their only option.

"Okay, tomorrow is our only chance; it's now or never!' Karl declared.

Rumors circulated that Germany was losing the war and that it was only a matter of time before the Americans moved in. No matter how hard Erich tried to talk them out of it, his words fell on deaf ears.

"You are going to get yourself killed. If it's true that the Americans are closing in on us, why not wait it out? Think about your family and loved ones waiting for you at the other end. It's just a matter of time; be patient!" Erich warned.

"Do you really think we'll get out of here alive? You've seen the horrors we witnessed; God knows it could be us tomorrow," a fellow prisoner exclaimed.

"If we lose the war, they'll get rid of us rather than let us fall into the hands of the Americans," another prisoner chimed in.

"What if we fall into the hands of the Russians?" another prisoner said.

"What if, what if! This is our only chance; it's now or never!" Karl replied angrily.

The following morning, just before dawn, the prisoners were abruptly awakened.

"Five minutes - gather your things; we're leaving in five minutes - schnell, schnell!" the SS guards shouted.

Herman and Karl's expressions conveyed everything – nothing but despair. Their only chance for escape had vanished, leaving them feeling trapped in a harsh environment where crimes against humanity exposed the depths of human cruelty. Erich was suddenly gripped by fear, sensing that this might be the end of the road for them.

The prisoners stepped out of their barracks, formed a line, and waited to be counted. They stood in the frigid morning air, shivering in their tattered clothing and clutching their meager belongings as they patiently awaited transport to their next destination.

When the SS guards came into view, Erich fixed his gaze on the ground, lost in thought as he tried to estimate how long he had been imprisoned. Since his arrest nearly two months ago, he had spent a few weeks at Gestapo headquarters and now over a month at Flossenbürg; it felt like an eternity.

"Is this it? Is this the end of the road for me?" his inner voice pondered.

The uncertainty of what lay ahead and the unknown future filled Erich with dread; he couldn't envision anything more brutal than what he and others had witnessed and endured at the hands of the SS guards and their commanding officers.

After what felt like an eternity, the SS head guard counted the prisoners for the third and final time as the other SS guards stood nearby, laughing and joking. Eventually, the prisoners were ordered onto the waiting trucks. Just like before, they were packed in like sardines, and despite the air being thick with the foul stench of unkempt bodies, the scent of fear was undeniable. A chilling silence hung in the air; the prisoners' nerves were on edge.

"So, this is it!" someone murmured.

"Silence," the SS guard yelled.

The SS guard peered into the truck, attempting to see who had spoken, but couldn't identify them.

Erich felt relieved to find Father Rudolph Schafer, Herman, and Karl in his group. Their friendship had become vital during these challenging times, helping them maintain their sanity. He was also relieved that Herman and Karl's escape plan didn't go according to plan; perhaps it wasn't meant to be. Recently, rumors have suggested that Germany was losing the war and that advancing U.S. troops were drawing closer. Erich held onto the hope that the rumors were true and that Maud would be waiting for him on the other side.

Later that day, they reached their destination, Dachau concentration camp.

"Schnell schnell," the SS guards shouted.

As the prisoners descended from the trucks, they were met by SS guards swinging their clubs at various angles. Just in time, Erich raised his arm to shield himself from a vicious blow aimed at his head. He felt blood oozing from his right ear and trickling down the side of his face. Erich's anger surged, and instinctively, he wanted to lash out, but he thought better of it. The tense atmosphere was undeniable. The SS guards seemed to be on edge, taking out their frustrations on the prisoners. Erich believed that even the SS guards might be anxious about whose hands they would end up in, especially with the Russians from the east advancing closer. Like everyone else, Erich hoped the Americans would come to their rescue.

CHAPTER 47

A Step Closer to Freedom – 1945

By late March 1945, news emerged that U.S. troops had crossed the Rhine at Oppenheim, dealing a significant blow to the German war effort. It was only a matter of time as the Americans advanced from the West while the Russians pushed from the East. Both the prisoners and the authorities at the prison camp worried about which hands they would end up in, the Russians or the Americans, with a preference for the latter.

It was late April when an emergency order at the Dachau concentration camp went into effect, requiring the evacuation of prisoners and staff within the next few days. Erich observed that the SS commandant and his senior associates had already departed, leaving the SS guards behind to carry out their orders.

"1, 2, 3, 4, 5..." the SS guard said as he paced back and forth, counting the prisoners.

Erich observed that the SS guards were noticeably tense and eager to leave as quickly as possible. After conducting a head count, the SS guards escorted the prisoners to the waiting school buses and trucks.

Erich sensed there was a chance they might be taken to the forest and executed. He imagined all of them being led into the forest, lined up, and shot! The night before, the prisoners had voiced their concerns, fearing this could be the end of the road for them. They contemplated various scenarios and decided they had nothing to lose but to fight until the end if necessary.

Erich and his fellow prisoners felt a sense of relief as they boarded a school bus, a welcome change from the cramped, dark confines of the truck. To their surprise, women and children also boarded the bus, and they soon learned that they were the family members of those involved in the failed assassination attempt on Hitler's life.

Once the bus was full, the SS guard announced that they would be taken to South Tyrol in northern Italy. Erich suspected and feared that this was merely a ploy, while in reality, they would soon be disposed of in a forest shortly after leaving the prison camp. To his immense relief, the bus passed by a dense forest and continued on, creating a great distance between the prisoners and the Dachau concentration camp. An hour or so into the journey, the landscape gave way to views of the countryside framed by snowcapped mountains, a welcome sight. Erich began to relax and surrendered himself to the gentle sway of the bus, lulling him into a sleepy state. When he woke up, he found the bus gradually winding its way up the mountainous pass.

The prisoners now made up of men, women, and children, began to relax. Erich hoped they would soon be in American hands. A few hours into the journey, they started to feel more at ease and began chatting among themselves, free from the guards' interruptions and shouts. Erich cautioned his fellow prisoners not to let their guard down, as they were still not out of the woods.

It was nearly midnight when they arrived at their destination, both tired and hungry. The SS guards handed over the prisoners to the regular German troops and left. Once the SS guards were out of sight, the prisoners felt a sense of relief at being free from their control. However, Erich had overheard the head SS guard giving the order:

"Kill all prisoners if captured by the Americans."

Erich's first thought was that up in this mountainous area, one could easily escape and hide.

Erich and his fellow prisoners were pleasantly surprised to find that their accommodation was in a large hotel by the lake. The hotel, which operated only during the summer months, was occupied by a few Luftwaffe generals and their staff. The prisoners received a warm welcome and were provided with food, water, and clean clothing - luxuries they sincerely appreciated.

The next morning, Erich awoke to breathtaking views of the crystal-clear aquamarine lake framed by snow-capped mountains, some reaching over 9,000 feet high. It was truly breathtaking. Erich enjoyed the freedom to explore the grounds without constant super-vision. This was a stark contrast to the previous barbed-wire prison camp, which was always under the watchful eyes of the armed SS guards. The regular guards, now in charge, treated the prisoners with the utmost respect, making them feel like valued guests.

When the American soldiers arrived at the hotel a few weeks later, the guards surrendered without a fight. Erich felt relieved that, whether due to a stroke of luck or a breakdown in communication between the SS guards and the regular guards, no harm came to the prisoners. The prisoners, along with the Luftwaffe generals, their staff, and the regular guards, were taken into protective custody by the Americans. Erich, like everyone else, felt a profound sense of relief, as falling into Russian hands meant a high likelihood of ending up in a Siberian prison camp.

The Americans then transferred the prisoners to Naples, where they underwent evaluation. The women and children were automatically returned to their homes, while non-Germans were repatriated to their countries of origin. Since Erich was an officer of the Abwehr, Germany's military intelligence service, he was viewed with suspicion. Together with other officers who opposed the Third Reich, Erich faced a thorough investigation. After a month, he was finally released. For Erich, it felt surreal to be free after months of captivity. His first thoughts were of Maud. After all, more than three years had passed since he bid her farewell at the train station in February 1942. Yet, somehow, it felt more recent. But before anything else, he needed to make his way back to Berlin.

CHAPTER 48

Berlin – June 1945

Following Adolf Hitler's suicide on April 30th, Berlin fell to Soviet forces on May 2nd. This came at a cost, as both sides - the Russians and the Germans - suffered heavy losses in their struggle against each other. After Russia's victory, Germany had no choice but to surrender unconditionally on May 7; the following day marked the end of World War II in Europe. Once the powerhouse of Europe, Germany has now been brought to its knees. By early June, French, American, and British forces arrived in Berlin, securing control of their respective territories.

For Erich, witnessing his beloved city divided into four districts by countries that were once regarded as enemies felt surreal: the East controlled by the Russians, the Southwest by the Americans, and the Western section by the French and British. He felt relieved that the war had ended, but he remained uncertain about what awaited his people. For now, it was a nation of displaced citizens under the control of their former enemies.

Erich's initial reaction upon returning to Berlin was one of dismay. Berlin, once a vibrant city, had now been reduced to rubble. What lay before him was a wasteland beyond recognition. He was also struck by the harsh realization that returning to his home in East Berlin was no longer an option, as he feared the Soviet forces would not allow him to leave; for all he knew, his apartment building could have been destroyed.

Despite the streets of Berlin being littered with burned-out vehicles and piles of rubble, Erich was struck by his people's resilience. The tram system was operating smoothly, with commuters boarding and disembarking, most of whom were men and women in business attire heading to the office. Mothers were out running errands with their children in tow, while others wandered the streets, appearing lost as if they couldn't grasp their situation.

In the heavily bombed areas, residents worked tirelessly alongside their neighbors to clear debris from their homes. Erich observed that it was predominantly women, children, and elderly men who stood in line, passing empty buckets in one direction and returning with buckets filled with debris. A few weeks earlier, it would have been these very same individuals who were left to defend their city against the advancing Russians, as most German men had either been killed in action or taken as prisoners of war. As Erich rounded the corner, he saw long lines of people waiting to fill their buckets at a public water source.

In the southwestern part of the city, Erich observed numerous American soldiers strolling down the streets, their postures relaxed and their movements unguarded – a stark contrast to an environment that had recently experienced conflict. Some walked happily arm in arm with local women, exchanging occasional glances that suggested love was in the air. However, for Erich, it felt surreal to see American soldiers on the streets of Berlin, especially since it seemed just recently that German soldiers had paraded through those same streets, celebrated as heroes. He recalled them moving like wind-up mechanical dolls, their boots pounding against the pavement; their mere presence commanded full and undivided attention. Additionally, the swastika flags that once adorned the buildings were no longer visible, a symbol that was once revered as sacred but was now tainted by evil. Erich knew all too well, after spending time at the concentration camps of Flossenbürg and Dachau, the depths to which human beings could sink. Germany must pay for this.

Erich was suddenly pulled from his thoughts by the sight of American trucks passing by, filled with German prisoners of war, including some high-ranking officers. He observed that the prisoners appeared relaxed and happy, laughing among themselves, undoubtedly relieved that the war was over and content to be in the custody of the Americans. Erich wondered whether these men had wielded power over others, sinking to a level of cruelty that he had both witnessed and experienced during his internment in the prison camps. One thing was clear: he was thankful for his freedom.

After a month in Berlin, Erich felt like a stranger in his once-beloved city, a place that had become unrecognizable and was now at the mercy of those previously seen as Germany's enemies. It was time for him to move on.

He reached out to his grandparents in Switzerland and felt relieved to learn that they were safe and healthy. They provided him with generous funds to enable him to travel to Ireland and, if necessary, beyond, for once he left Berlin, there would be no turning back. Despite being apart from Maud for more than three years, Erich had never stopped thinking about her, yet doubts crept into the back of his mind: what if? The only way for him to find out was by going to Ireland. If Maud had moved on, he could go to America.

CHAPTER 49

Late Summer of 1945

It was a beautiful late summer day, with clear blue skies and unexpectedly warm weather. Heavy rain was predicted for the coming days, making the gathering and storing of hay important. The workers' children enjoyed playing on the haystacks until they were shooed away and sent home. By 9 p.m., the hay was collected, covered with tarps, and weighed down with stones.

Maud and her mother were exhausted after assisting Patrick and Margaret all day. Since dawn, they had helped Margaret prepare enough food to feed the neighbors who came to gather the hay.

"Will I have the pleasure of your company later?" Patrick asked Maud and Sheila.

"Thanks, Patrick. I think I'll call it a night. I need to get this little one to bed; he's exhausted," Maud replied.

Maud bent down to pick up little Erich, who seemed tired since it was well past his bedtime.

"Ah, he has a fine head of hair, just like his dad," Patrick said as he leaned in to ruffle the boy's hair.

"Wherever you are, Erich, I know you're out there somewhere. Please, please come home," Patrick added.

They all stood in silence for a moment.

Maud and Sheila had just settled at the kitchen table with cups of tea in hand when they heard a knock on the door. They exchanged glances, curious about who might be calling so late at night.

"It's a bit late to be calling at this hour. Who on earth could it be? I hope they aren't expecting to be entertained; I'm exhausted and ready for bed," Sheila said.

Another knock came louder this time, followed by a third knock that sounded more urgent.

"It's all right, Mum. I'll get it," Maud said as she stood up and walked toward the hallway to answer the door.

"I'm coming, I'm coming – hold your horses," Maud said wearily as she opened the door.

To Maud's surprise, Erich stood on the other side of the door. Instinctively, her hand flew to her mouth; she was speechless. She didn't know whether to laugh or to cry.

"Who is it, Maud?" Sheila called as she approached the door, eager to find out who might be calling at such a late hour.

Sheila stepped back as if she had just seen a ghost.

"Lord, merciful God! We were just talking about you. Your ears must have been burning," Sheila said, laughing nervously.

They all paused for a moment, unsure about what to say next.

"You'd better come in, love, before we all pass out from the shock," Sheila said, breaking the awkward moment of silence.

Maud, Sheila, and Erich stood in the kitchen, at a loss for words. After all, more than three years had passed without knowing whether Erich was dead or alive, and now he had unexpectedly turned up out of the blue.

"I think I'll head off to bed now and leave you two. You have a lot of catching up to do. Oh, it's wonderful to see you, Erich," Sheila said, gently squeezing Erich's arm.

Maud and Erich stood there for a moment, taking each other in. Then, they spoke at the same time.

"No, you go ahead," Maud said with a giggle.

"My darling Maud, I realize this is a lot for you to take in. It has been over three years since we last saw each other, and now I stand before you. I would fully understand if you have moved on with someone else," Erich said, stepping closer and gently taking Maud's hands in his.

Erich had envisioned their reunion countless times, but he remained realistic; after all, they hadn't seen each other in a long time, and the only communication he had received from her was a telegram confirming that she had arrived safely in Ireland. He vividly recalled seeing Maud off at the Berlin train station in February 1942. Yet, standing in the kitchen with Maud, it felt as though it had only been recent, despite the significant amount of time that had passed.

During those years apart, he never lost hope of seeing her again. One of his biggest fears was that Maud believed he was dead and had moved on. The worst-case scenario would have been if she had begun a new life with someone else, but he felt reassured when he called at the house and found only Maud and her mother there. The mere thought of another man answering the door would have devastated him. Now that he was here, he realized they had much catching up to do.

"Oh, my love, I've hoped and prayed that someday you would show up," Maud said.

She reached out and gently touched Eric's face before kissing him softly.

"Maud, I've missed you so much. I thought this day would never come," Eric said, filled with emotion.

He then took her in his arms and held her tightly, lifting her off her feet and not wanting to let her go.

After a while, they both stood there, taking each other in.

"You must be hungry; I'll get you something to eat," Maud said.

Erich pulled her back into his arms and kissed her tenderly.

"I never gave up on you. I knew you were out there somewhere," Maud said, her voice filled with emotion as tears began to well up in her eyes.

"We heard about the prison camps and what they did to the Jews," she added.

"Darling, I've been in such camps, and it was hell. The only thing that kept me alive was you," Erich said, embracing her tightly as if he never wanted to let her go.

"Mama, Mama," a little boy cried, running into the room and wondering who this stranger was that his mother was embracing.

His cry startled Erich and reminded Maud that she had forgotten to mention their son.

"Erich, it's okay, sweetheart. There's no need to be afraid," Maud said as she knelt down and embraced her son.

"Erich, this is your father," Maud said, turning to look at Erich as she comforted their son.

"That day you saw me off at the train station, I was pregnant, but I didn't find out until a month later," Maud said to Erich, reaching out to touch his arm.

"I wrote to you, but I guess you never received my letter," she added.

"You've named him after me," Erich said, astonished.

Upon hearing this news, tears welled up in his eyes.

Holding her son in her arms, Maud stepped forward and embraced Erich. They both sobbed with joy at their reunion, and Erich was filled with emotion upon discovering he had a son.

The End

Made in the USA
Las Vegas, NV
13 September 2025

27866244R00132